WAR GAMES

RITVIK KUKREJA

Srishti
Publishers & Distributors

Srishti Publishers & Distributors
A unit of AJR Publishing LLP
212A, Peacock Lane
Shahpur Jat, New Delhi – 110 049

editorial@srishtipublishers.com

First published by
Srishti Publishers & Distributors in 2025

Copyright © Ritvik Kukreja, 2025

10 9 8 7 6 5 4 3 2 1

This is a work of fiction. The characters, places, organisations and events described in this book are either a work of the author's imagination or have been used fictitiously. Any resemblance to people, living or dead, places, events, communities or organisations is purely coincidental.

The author asserts the moral right to be identified as the author of this work.

All rights reserved. No part of this publication may be reproduced, stored in a retrieval system, or transmitted, in any form or by any means, electronic, mechanical, photocopying, recording or otherwise, without the prior written permission of the Publishers.

Printed and bound in India.

Many jihadists believe in a fable that if they die as martyrs, they will be rewarded with seventy-two eternal virgins in heaven. But if killed by a woman, they will be sent straight to hell.

Prologue
Bullet Rain

Present Day
Syria

Handcuffed and blindfolded by tattered cloth strips, Arjan, a young man, knelt on the ground, dishevelled and battered. Beads of sweat streaking his pale, stubbled face glistened in the relentless desert sun. To his sides, two other hapless captives, Ahmed and Ron, shared his grim fate, all dressed in Guantanamo-inspired orange jumpsuits.

The macabre stage was set: six militiamen, shrouded in black garbs and balaclavas, orchestrated the grotesque spectacle of a filmed execution. With a high-definition camera poised to capture the killings and a massive green screen masking the desolate locale, the execution site bore an uncanny resemblance to a shoddy movie set.

"*Allah hu Akbar!*" fervent chants pierced through the eerie silence as militiamen, wielding assault rifles, took up positions behind the captives. Arjan could feel his heart slamming against his ribcage. Without warning, the executioners opened fire. The Kalashnikov assault rifles erupted with a rumbling roar. Bullets tore into the sky, spewing trails of acrid smoke while the spent casings crashed to the ground. Amidst this tumult, the militiamen jeered raucously at the trembling captives. Unamused by the theatrics, the field commander, a stocky bespectacled figure, raised his hand to bring the hysterics to an abrupt end. His intense, hooded brown eyes held a gravity that cut through the air, swiftly restoring solemnity to the affair.

Sobering up, the militiamen fell back into their positions and proceeded to reload their weapons. The sharp clinks of ammunition resounded through the tense atmosphere. With each passing moment, the captives' ordeal deepened, the agonizing wait stretching to its breaking point. Beneath the tight blindfold, Arjan squeezed his eyes shut and whispered a prayer under his breath. After a prolonged delay, the thugs leveled their guns once more at the captives. Their fingers hovered over the triggers as they awaited the cameraman's cue.

The cameraman panned his lens, visibly underwhelmed by the mise-en-scène. Looking up, he bellowed, "Spread out a little. You don't want a bloodbath, do you?"

The executioners yanked the captives by the scruff of their necks, forcefully repositioning them until they were about four feet apart.

The cameraman peered through the viewfinder again, signaling approval with a brisk thumbs-up. "*Mashallah*," he muttered.

Arjan's heartbeat quickened as the muzzle of the assault rifle pressed against the back of his head.

The cameraman punched the record button and called out, "Rolling."

A profound sense of dread overcame the captives, who, in that chilling moment, let go of their souls.

"Who's up first?" the cameraman enquired, seeking to fine-tune his focus accordingly.

"Let's keep it a surprise… so, who's it gonna be?" a voice echoed, laced with a disturbing sense of schadenfreude.

"It's like Russian roulette," another voice chortled, "Except all of you die."

The militiamen erupted into another bout of laughter, which was abruptly punctuated by a gunshot. Arjan skipped a beat. With a sickening thud, Ahmed collapsed lifeless, his skull shattered, blood spilling onto the parched ground. Arjan and Ron, numb with dread, could no longer bear the anticipation. On his turn, Arjan's executioner cocked the gun.

Arjan's body tensed up, bracing for the inevitable. Clenching his fists and gritting his teeth, he steeled himself for the final moment as the executioner pulled the trigger halfway. BOOM!

A thunderous blast ripped through the dunes. The camera tumbled, and empty bullet casings on the blood-soaked sand filled its frame before everything faded into a blackout.

1
Squad Aces

Five months earlier
New Delhi

Foam bullets lay strewn across the marble floor of a plush bedroom. A fifty-five-inch TV loomed above a shelf cluttered with action figurines and novels. A Nerf gun lay askew at the edge, its barrel clutching a jammed bullet that never found its mark. Arjan sat hunched over his gaming setup, his fingers absently tracing the surface of his keyboard. The neon glow from his multi-monitor rig spilled into the room, faint and steady, like the pulse of a restless heart. On the desk, an ornate frame held a photo of him and Priya, their smiles frozen in a distant moment. The buzz of his phone broke the silence. Arjan grabbed it, his hope fading when he saw the name on the screen.

Not Priya, just Sahin. *'Streaming today?'* the message read.

'Don't feel like it. Maybe tomorrow,' he typed back.

Sahin's reply arrived instantly, *'Bro, no stream means no buzz. Only two days to go. Please don't bail on us.'*

His message was capped by a funny meme, one of their inside jokes that tugged a reluctant smile from Arjan. The brief exchange felt like a nudge, drawing him back to his virtual world, where he had superpowers. With a quiet resolve, Arjan straightened up, brushing his lingering thoughts aside. He raked a hand through his mussed-up hair, then slipped on his headset, angling the microphone into place. His hand hesitated over the 'go-live' button, nerves tingling.

With a deep breath and steady hand, he clicked. The screen lit up, and his voice started measured, careful. "Hi, I'm Arjan, twenty-one, tuning in from New Delhi for my first livestream." Then, as if a switch flipped, confidence burst forth, his smile settling in place. "I can't wait to introduce you to my gaming squad, but before we dive in, let's zoom out and talk about something bigger – gaming itself. It's a billion-dollar industry, yet some still dismiss it as child's play; a waste of time. Well, let me set the record straight: Everyone's a gamer, whether they realize it or not."

He sat back, letting the words settle before leaning in again, fully in his element now. "Sounds too sweeping? Picture this: a schoolteacher on your metro ride, swiping through Clash of Clans like her kingdom depends on it. Or a burnt-out corporate dude on a flight, pounding Street Fighter combos like he's taking out his boss. What would you call them, huh?"

His grin grew wider, the examples spilling out faster. "Even your grandparents solving Sudoku to keep dementia at bay. From toddlers on iPads to real-life soldiers on training simulators – gaming doesn't discriminate. Whether you're crushing candies or slaying dragons, you're already part of a universe you didn't even know you belonged to."

Arjan paused, setting his water down and wiping his mouth with the back of his hand. "Video games are more than just a pastime. They're an escape. A portal to worlds where the rules of reality don't apply – no baggage, no problems weighing you down."

The photo frame crept at the edge of his vision, pulling at his focus. "At least for a while," he murmured.

He pressed on, his tone picking up again, "And modern-day video games? They've taken it to a whole new level. You're not just escaping alone; you're playing alongside real people from every corner of the world. Isn't that incredible? For all we know, that schoolteacher on the metro could be raiding a Japanese teenager's outpost, while an autorickshaw driver waiting for his next fare could be locked in a tense Ludo match with a French businesswoman. How fascinating is that?"

His eyes glinted with a hint of awe. "And it only gets better – you don't just play; you connect. You forge friendships. These are the new-age pen pals, people you may never meet, yet they become a part of your world." He paused, a faint smile brushing his lips.

"I know this because I've lived it. I've made friends with some incredible people while playing online, and they've become more than just teammates – they are my virtual family. We call ourselves the Squad Aces. We may be scattered across the globe, and sure, we've never met in person, but the bond we've built? It's as real as it gets."

He sat back slightly, his voice steady and proud. "In just two years, we've clinched seven online championships, and now we're on the cusp of something even bigger. Here's the deal: the World Gaming Championship is just around the corner. It's the biggest esports event on the planet, and we're right in the thick of it. If we win the next two qualifier matches, we're off to Germany. We'll finally meet and play side by side in the grand finale at the iconic Munich gaming arena. And the cherry on top? A shot at a million-dollar prize!"

He let the words hang for a moment, giving them space to resonate. Arjan's eyes flicked to his streaming overlay, catching the viewer count: seventy-two and climbing. A flutter of excitement, like a passing butterfly, stirred in his stomach. His tone softened as he leaned closer to the mic. "To get you hyped for the championship, we've put together something special – a brief introduction video that goes beyond gameplay or records. It's a window into our everyday lives, a chance for you to see the squad as we really are. Not just players but people with stories, struggles, and victories of our own. So, come along as we pull back the curtain and show you the real faces behind the avatars."

Arjan minimized the stream and started the screen-sharing function on his computer. He moved his cursor over the 'squad-intro.mp4' file on the desktop. With a click, the video swelled across the screen while Arjan's livestream shrank into a small Picture-in-Picture window tucked in the corner. As it played, Arjan settled into the role of both spectator and narrator. His eyes attentively followed the scenes, ready to provide insights and weave a narrative that would bring his viewers closer to the personal worlds of his team members.

The video kicked off with the high-octane action of the German Grand Prix, the air crackling with the roar of turbocharged engines and a captivated crowd. Amid the blur of speeding cars, a white Ferrari suddenly broke away from the pack, veering off the tarmac and screeching into the pitstop. Mechanics swarmed the car like clockwork – stabilizing it, wiping the driver's visor, and bolting on fresh tires in an instant. The camera zoomed in on Eitan, a curly-haired Caucasian guy in a fireproof suit. With a nod, he sent the car roaring back onto the track. As the crew dispersed, Eitan turned to the camera. "Hi, I am Eitan. I am twenty-four. In the real world, I'm a Formula One mechanic. In the virtual world, I'm the squad's armorer."

Eitan's introduction wrapped up, and Arjan's voice chimed in, taking on a nasal note. "Crafting armour in the chaos of gunfights demands composure and surgeon-like precision – skills Eitan mastered in the high-pressure pits of Formula One. It's what gives him a distinct edge in the game."

While the video queued up for the next intro, Arjan reached into a drawer beside him. He picked out an Otrivin spray from a small stash and delivered a few quick pumps into his nostrils with practiced ease. A sigh of relief escaped him as he settled back into his seat.

On-screen, the frenetic energy of the Grand Prix melted away, giving way to a scene of striking contrast. Under the unrelenting Arabian sun, the camera panned to the tranquil scene outside the Masjid al-Haram in Mecca, where pilgrims in white moved in hushed reverence.

The focus shifted to Faiz, clad in pristine white *Ihram*. He stood with quiet composure, his stubbled face softening into a warm smile as he met the camera's gaze. "Hi! I'm Faiz. I'm nineteen, a computer engineering student, and in the game world, I play as a medic," he said, an understated confidence behind his words.

Arjan's voiceover kicked in, brimming with admiration and praise. "Faiz is the definition of a team player. If you're knocked down mid-fight, Doctor Faiz will find you, revive you and get you back into action."

A live comment from a viewer popped up beside the livestream overlay: *'Did you know? As a non-Muslim, you are forbidden to even enter Mecca.'*

Arjan paused briefly, his tone steady as he addressed it. "Yes, Mr FatBatman53, I'm aware of that. And that, right there, is the beauty of online gaming. Without it, Faiz and I might have never crossed paths."

As Faiz's segment concluded with clips of him engaging warmly with locals, Arjan's voice returned, this time carrying a playful edge. "Here's a fun tidbit for you all: Faiz is also an ethical hacker. Surprising, right? But hey, having someone on your team with those skills can be super handy. You never know when we might need them!"

The scene shifted to Lahore, a bustling metropolis alive with vibrant chaos. The camera swept across the urban sprawl before it settled on Minar-e-Pakistan, where traffic swirled like a restless river. "In case you're wondering, we didn't shoot these slick aerials. Credit goes to the internet – the gift that keeps on giving," Arjan quipped, a sly smile in his voice.

The view cut to a modest, lived-in apartment. Zafar, a middle-aged tubby guy, lounged in a threadbare recliner as he played a video game. On-screen, his avatar was knee-deep in mayhem – likely a result of his own questionable gameplay. Yet Zafar, unbothered, casually turned away from the screen to munch on fried chicken wings.

"Jeez! The sheer sight of those greasy fingers clutching the controller is sending my OCD into a meltdown," Arjan groused, squirming in his chair.

As the game ended, Zafar turned toward the docked camera. "Hey there! I'm Zafar. In-game, I take on the role of an explosives expert, specializing in weapons of mass destruction. Pretty thrilling, right? In real life, though, I work a not-so-explosive job in telecommunications." Zafar grabbed a swig of Diet Coke and dove back into the game.

"What do I say about this guy?" Arjan chimed in, his voice laced with amused exasperation. "To be honest, when I was writing this intro, I tried to link everyone's real-life traits to their gaming style, you know, to make it sound all cool and poetic. But with Zafar? I hit a wall. He is so… unconventional. A total wild card."

Just then, a baby's cries echoed in the background. Without missing a beat, Zafar's gamer instincts were replaced by paternal ones. Navigating a minefield of scattered Lego pieces, he scooped up his toddler from the cot and pacified her with the tenderness of a doting father.

"Oh! Did I mention Zafar's a father of two? Yeah, he's a gamer dad – juggling work, diaper duties, and gaming like a pro."

Cradling her in one arm, he settled back into the recliner and grabbed the controller. The in-game fireworks lit up the screen, mesmerizing her into silence.

As the scene shifted away from Zafar's apartment, Arjan's voice summed up with fond affection, "Though I couldn't find a textbook trait for Zafar, I did find something priceless – a reminder that, in the end, gaming's all about having a blast. Sometimes, quite literally!"

Before moving on to the next player, Arjan addressed some comments on the fly. "For those of you commenting on how we get along since Zafar is Pakistani, let me tell you, this divide has never soured our bond." A beat later, he continued, "Not gonna lie, though, the camaraderie gets seriously tested when India and Pakistan clash on the cricket field," deftly easing the seriousness of the question.

The next comment read, *'Israeli, Arab, Pakistani, and Indian on the same team. Is this a freaking gaming squad or an inter-faith brotherhood crusade?'* Although the roasting comment initially ruffled Arjan, he couldn't help but silently admire the wits of the keyboard warrior. In a discreet attempt to avoid drawing attention to the jibe, he gracefully remarked, "More questions later, it's almost time to meet our MVP."

The scene shifted to Sahin without any extravagant drone shots, delving straight into his room. Cloaked in a black hoodie, Sahin was deeply immersed in a video game, the dim light of his room casting shadows as he took sips of black coffee. With a lean frame, his face remained a mystery, skillfully obscured by a Photoshop filter, only deepening his enigmatic aura.

"This is Sahin," Arjan commented, his tone shifting to one of reverence. "At the risk of sounding like a total fanboy, let me say it – this guy is a legend. Not just my favourite, he's everyone's favourite. He's the freaking GOAT."

"What?" Arjan shrugged. "I warned you I'm a fanboy."

On screen, Sahin's avatar glided through the game like a phantom, landing perfect headshots with effortless grace.

"In real life," Arjan rambled on, "Sahin is as elusive as he is in-game. No one's seen him or heard him. A little mystery in an age of over-exposure? Refreshing, right?" He paused, then deadpanned, "Not! It's a nightmare. Especially when you're in the middle of tactical discussions and he's radio silent. Still, he's too good to bench. Most geniuses have their eccentricities, and Sahin's no exception."

As Sahin's character continued to dominate the game, Arjan's tone softened, turning reflective. "For all his quirks, I'd like to think we've built something rare – a bond that just clicks in its own unconventional way," he admitted. "We text a lot, and – believe it or not – you can talk to him about anything. It's like he's cracked the code to our greatest mysteries: the meaning of life, the secret to understanding women, you name it. I keep joking he could have an alternate career as a motivational guru if he weren't so private."

He paused for effect, a grin playing at his lips. "And here's the real kicker: Sahin was ranked the world's number one gamer last year."

The revelation landed like a mic drop, followed by breathtaking shots of New Delhi, the beautiful capital, steeped in centuries of history and culture. The visuals then returned to familiar ground – Arjan's room, the heart of his command centre. Fiddling with the hem of his designer T-shirt, he drew back his shoulders and met the camera with an easy smile. "Last, but definitely not least – spoiler alert – it's me, Arjan. *Naam toh suna hoga.* Captain of Squad Aces and in-game aggressor…"

Before he could finish, a blur of golden fur burst into the frame, landing squarely in his lap. Laughing, Arjan ruffled the dog's ears, "Oh, right! Meet Mario – our unofficial mascot and resident video-bomber. Whether I'm raging a loss, the game's lagging, or my shots refuse to land – he's the one who keeps me sane."

Mario wagged his tail on cue, earning a loving belly rub.

Arjan glanced back into the camera, his tone warm. "Thanks a lot for tuning in and getting to know the Squad Aces. Don't forget to like, share, and subscribe – you know the drill." Just as he reached to turn off the webcam, his hand paused mid-air, his expression turning earnest. "Oh, and one last thing – our first qualifier match is in two days, live on the official WGC channel. I'll drop all the details in the description below. So set those reminders and join us for what's going to be an action-packed game." With a quick salute, Arjan signed off. As the stream ended, he leaned back in his chair, exhaling slowly. Two hundred viewers, a steady stream of comments, and a handful of new subscribers – it should have felt like a win.

But as the monitors dimmed, the energy in the room began to shift. The room seemed to expand around him, the lingering adrenaline of the virtual world fading too quickly. For a moment, the silence was almost soothing until it gave way to a familiar, gnawing ache. His gaze drifted to his phone, hesitation stretching thin before he finally gave in. His fingers moved quickly, the words forming as though they'd been waiting too long. With a deep breath, he pressed send, and for a second, the weight on his chest eased. Then his phone buzzed and hope flared. Arjan grabbed it eagerly, only to see a flood of notifications from his concluded stream. His chest tightened as he swiped back to WhatsApp, scanning the screen for her name. The message sat there, stuck on the dreaded single tick. Stalled, much like their relationship. He stared at the screen until the letters blurred, then tossed the phone onto the bed. He lay back, his eyes fixed on the ceiling, as the silence settled over him – heavier, colder than before.

2
Strawberry Generation

The opulent dining room basked in the morning sunlight, its rays casting a warm glow over the marble floors and lavish decor. Seated at the monolithic dining table, Rajesh, a burly man in his fifties with a distinguished mustache, was engrossed in a newspaper. From the kitchen, the soft strains of a devotional bhajan floated through the air, mingling with the mouthwatering aroma of parathas in the making. However, the ambiance shifted abruptly the moment Rajesh took a sip of his tea. A look of disgust contorted his face. He set the cup down with disdain and pushed it away. "Raju! Get me a fresh cup of tea!" His command echoed through the room.

Moments later, Anita, a graceful middle-aged woman, emerged from the kitchen followed by Raju, the house-help who carried the serving plate.

"Piping hot aloo parathas," Anita announced cheerfully, although her effervescence was at odds with Rajesh's sullen mood.

"Woh sab toh theek hai. Sahab-zaade kahaan hai?" (His Highness is still sleeping?) Rajesh inquired, peering over the newspaper.

"Let it go. He must have slept late." Anita laid a table mat in front of Rajesh for Raju to set the plate on.

Rajesh's discontent simmered as Anita fetched a box of medicine from the lacquered sideboard.

"This kid has no future. It'll be too late before he realizes," he muttered. His voice rose in intensity as he went on, "Kids these days don't have fire in their bellies. They are handed everything on a silver platter."

"I said let it go. Why raise your blood pressure?" she advised.

Just as Rajesh was about to dig into the crispy paratha, Anita handed him a tablet and a glass of water.

With a swift gulp of water, he downed the medicine, his discomfort evident as he muttered, "Pass me an antacid, the heartburn is unbearable."

Just then, Raju arrived with a freshly brewed pot of tea and placed it on the table.

"It's your fifth cup of tea since morning. You're asking for acidity," Anita said shaking her head.

"Fifth? I sent at least two cups back. Doesn't count," Rajesh retorted.

"You've had enough for now," Anita insisted, sitting down beside him and pouring herself a cup.

"I'll decide when I've had enough," Rajesh said, reaching for the pot.

"Fine, but don't complain later."

The squabble between them succeeded where several alarms had failed – it roused Arjan out of his deep slumber. Arjan opened his eyes and glanced at the clock. "Shit!" he groaned, casting the blanket aside and leaping out of bed. Rushing through a quick shower, he ripped a black tee and a pair of jeans off their hangers, yanking them on in a hurry.

Moments later, he stormed out of his room and made a beeline for the main door, pausing just long enough to greet his parents, "Good morning, folks."

"At least have something for breakfast..." Anita called after him.

"Sorry, Mumma, I am running late! See you later," Arjan said, slinging a backpack over his shoulder and snatching up his car keys. Just as he flung the main door open, Rajesh growled from behind the newspaper, "Arjan! Come back. I want to talk to you."

His voice left no room for negotiation.

Arjan winced and stopped short. Skipping the lecture – where Priya was sure to be – was out of the question but so was ignoring his father's call.

Glancing at his wristwatch, he muttered under his breath, "Of all days…" With a reluctant sigh, he closed the door, retraced his steps, and dragged himself toward the dining table.

"Take a seat," Rajesh said, lowering the newspaper just enough to pin Arjan with a stern gaze.

Arjan slowly pulled a chair and settled in it.

"That's my good boy," Anita teased, already rising to her feet. "Let me get you some hot parathas."

"No, Mumma. I don't have time to eat. I'm really late. Anyway, I'm on a diet these days."

"*Achha?* And all that junk that you eat through the night? I'm sure that's super healthy!"

Arjan shook his head subtly, his brows knitting together in a quiet plea for his mother not to arm his father with more ammunition.

Suppressing a chuckle at her son's predicament, Anita relented. "Never mind," she said with a grin, "I'll get you some fresh fruits then." With a playful wink, she turned on her heel and disappeared into the kitchen.

Meanwhile, Rajesh folded the newspaper and set it aside, his eyes narrowing as he focused on Arjan. "Why did you wake up so late? Didn't you set your alarm?"

"Papa, I was streaming a video game last night," Arjan stated matter-of-factly.

"Are you twelve? When will you stop wasting time on childish video games?"

"Papa! It's not child's play," Arjan said, leaning forward with conviction. "Video game streamers earn a lot. Take PewDiePie for example – the Swedish gamer with millions of subscribers. He earns millions!"

Rajesh paused mid-bite, his frown deepening. "Wait. People sit and watch someone else play video games? Games they could play themselves?"

"Well... yeah," Arjan said, hesitating. "I mean, some of them even pay to watch."

"What?" Rajesh cut in, setting down his paratha and looking at Arjan in sheer disbelief. "You're telling me people pay real money to watch someone... click buttons?"

"Take it as any other sport! It takes skills, strategies..."

Rajesh let out a long, dramatic sigh, shaking his head. "God bless this generation."

Knowing he had to hit harder, Arjan leaned in, determined. "Esports championships offer bigger prize money than Wimbledon, Papa! There's serious scope in it."

Rajesh scoffed, tearing off a piece of paratha and dunking it into the yogurt with deliberate slowness, as if trying to process the madness. "And what are the odds you'll be as famous as this... Eww-goo-guy?"

"Papa! It's Pew-Die-Pie."

"Doesn't matter. It doesn't make sense either way," Rajesh replied bluntly. Leaning forward, he asked, "How many subscribers do you have?"

Eager to sidestep the uncomfortable question, Arjan swiftly pushed back his chair, excusing himself, "Papa, I really got to go. I'm already late for an important lecture."

"If you were so worried about being late, you should've gotten up on time."

As usual, his father was right. Arjan had woken up so late that he was never going to make it to the lecture anyway. Dropping his eyes, Arjan sat resignedly back down.

After a brief pause, Rajesh asked, "So what was I asking?"

"Ten," Arjan mumbled.

"What?"

"You asked how many subscribers I have?"

"Oh!" Rajesh paused to sip away the last of his tea, then continued,

"You stayed up all night for ten subscribers," dismissing Arjan's dedication with a wry smirk.

"But I'm only getting started," Arjan defended.

"Grow up! How can you turn a futile hobby into a career? You've got to have a plan in life!"

"I do have a plan, Papa. I am doing journalism as a backup too."

"Ek course kar lene se journalist nahi ban jaate. Jab sarhad pe jaane ko bolenge toh jaa paaoge? Hogi himmat?" (A journalism course won't make you a journalist. What will you do when you're asked to cover a war? Would you have the courage?)

"Papa! Har baat mein 'sarhad' kyu aa jaati hai?" (Why do you bring up 'the battlefield' in every argument?)

"Kyuki asli zindagi ka maidaan kissi yudh kshetra se kam nahi," (Because the battlefield of real life is no less ruthless than any war zone,) Rajesh remarked, his words carrying the weight of a lifetime's experience.

Arjan parted his lips, but before he could speak, Rajesh slid the newspaper across the table. The bold headline glared up at Arjan: *Islamic State beheads American Journalist.*

Arjan froze. His throat went dry as he scanned the chilling words. He pushed the newspaper aside, shaking his head. "It's… it's horrifying. But what does that have to do with me?"

"Papa! Main Iraq thodi jaa raha hoon!" (I'm not going to Iraq!) Arjan exclaimed, his voice bleeding frustration.

Rajesh sighed, shaking his head. "It's not about that. What I'm trying to say is… you haven't thought this through. Whether it's your primary plan or this so-called backup, neither makes sense to me." He paused, his tone softening slightly. "See, I get the whole 'follow your heart' thing, but don't let your brain go on a long vacation."

Arjan leaned forward, his voice insistent. "Not every journalism student has to become a war correspondent. There are plenty of other beats that one can pursue like sports, politics, entertainment. At least give me a chance to prove myself."

"Hmm… fair enough. So, what do you want to pursue?"

Caught off guard, Arjan looked away before responding, "Well, I am still deciding."

Shaking his head in disappointment, Rajesh said, "You're as aimless as Ritwik Roshan in *Lakshya* – chasing what looks cool but with no real direction or clarity. At least he figured it out eventually. When will you?"

Arjan's lips pressed into a thin line as his gaze fell, the flicker of something unspoken passing across his face before it vanished.

Rajesh clasped his hands tightly in front of him, "Yours is a strawberry generation," he said, his tone sharp. "Bruises way too easily. You don't get it because you've been living a privileged life. But we won't be around forever to pick up the pieces when things fall apart."

As Anita emerged from the kitchen carrying an artfully arranged fruit platter, Arjan sat in silent acquiescence.

"I am still advising you to join my business. Stop wasting your time."

"Arrey, will you cut him some slack? At least let him have breakfast in peace," Anita interjected.

Arjan, avoiding his father's gaze, sheepishly plucked a strawberry from the platter and nibbled on it, as if stalling for time.

Meanwhile, Rajesh leaned back, pushing away from the table to rise from his chair. He reached for the blazer draped over the backrest and slipped it on in one smooth motion. As he prepared to leave, he couldn't resist taking a parting shot at his son. "*Ab aise aisho-aaram se jeena hai, toh hum dono mein se kissi ek ko toh mehnat karni padegi. Chalo! Main hi laga rehta hoon.*" (If we have to maintain such lavish lifestyle, then one of us has to put in the hard work. Let me be the one to keep slogging).

Arjan, keeping his chin tucked against his chest, absorbed the stark reality laid bare by his father.

As Rajesh strode away, Anita reassured Arjan with a gentle touch on his shoulder. "Don't take Papa's harsh words to heart. He cares deeply about you,"

Arjan gave a silent nod, his thoughts adrift as his gaze lifted to the clock. *Priya must have left by now*, he thought with a quiet sigh, idly pushing the cut fruits around on his plate.

After a moment of observing his sluggish eating, Anita asked, "Arjan, aren't you running late?"

"No point hurrying now. Papa has already made me miss an important lecture," Arjan said sombrely.

"Well, that works perfectly for me. Drop me off on the way then," Anita suggested with a smile.

"Where?"

"I have a kitty party at eleven,"

"*Nahi yaar*," Arjan offered a feeble protest.

"*Bas mein gayi aur aa gayi* (I'll be ready in no time). You're the world's best son," Anita teased, blowing a flying kiss his way as she headed off to get ready.

Arjan sighed, shaking his head with a resigned smile. "Every time," he muttered.

Just then, his phone buzzed. Arjan glanced at the screen lazily, but the moment his eyes landed on the sender's name, his breath caught – Priya. Finally.

His fingers fumbled as he hurried to open the message. The moment he read it, the colour drained from his face. For what felt like an eternity, he sat there frozen, staring blankly at the screen as the world around him blurred into silence.

3
No Ace Left Behind

In the moments leading up to the big game, Arjan sat frozen before his dormant gaming rig. His phone buzzed relentlessly with messages from his squad mates, urging him to come online. Privy to his personal upheaval, they feared Arjan might not show up. With only two minutes to kick-off, Arjan rose from his chair, ignoring the notifications clamoring for his attention. Without so much as a glance at his phone, he walked away, leaving it untouched on the desk.

The rest of the Squad Aces, unsettled by Arjan's absence, stepped into the arena – a virtual battleground set on the mythical island of Halcyon. Their avatars, clad in gothic plate armour adorned with blue mantlings, faced off against Team Nucleus, whose avatars bore orange accents. Each avatar proudly displayed their team insignia on the chest plate of their iron cuirass. Above them, like radiant halos, their gamer-tags, enclosed in glowing brackets < >, hovered brightly, marking their identities in the digital fray. As part of the pre-game ritual, both teams boarded their respective Viking ships, ready to be ferried toward the medieval castle – the epicentre of the impending clash.

"Welcome to the qualifiers of the World Gaming Championship 2014!" the commentator's voice boomed. "It's Squad Aces versus Team Nucleus, a showdown with a bit of bad blood. Last year, Nucleus knocked the Aces out in the league stages. Now, Nucleus looks to replicate their dominance, while the Aces are hungry to exact long-awaited revenge." As the on-screen clock counted down, tension in the virtual arena reached a fever pitch.

Stuck in the real world, Arjan stood at the bathroom sink, splashing cold water onto his face. His eyes closed briefly as he gripped the edge of the countertop, wrestling with his inner turmoil. This wasn't just a game, it was about being there for the team that had always counted on him, no matter what.

With sudden resolve, he stepped out of the bathroom, droplets still clinging to his cheeks. He snatched up the ornate frame from his desk and tossed it into the trash can. The metallic clank rang through the room with a sharp sense of finality. Arjan sat down, powered up his rig and squared his shoulders. As his avatar plunged into the virtual world, he swiftly spritzed nasal spray into his nostrils, ensuring clarity for the chaos ahead.

As the Viking ships set sail, Arjan's avatar spawned into the game.

"Thank God you're here!" Faiz exclaimed in the chat, his tension palpable. "We really thought you'd abandoned us!"

Arjan's voice was steady as he invoked their squad's motto, "One squad, one mind, no Ace left behind." His fingers moved deftly across the controller as he outfitted his avatar, <Arjan>, with a formidable loadout.

"Better late than never, skipper," Faiz replied, his relief evident.

Upon spotting <Arjan>, Sahin's avatar leaped up in excitement and reached out for a high-five. The rest of the team followed suit, their avatars converging into a tight cluster in a virtual team huddle.

Arjan addressed his teammates with a steely conviction, "Best of luck, everyone. We've waited a whole year for this moment. Let's make it count!"

His powerful voice ignited a fire within the team as its avatars disembarked on the shores and stormed the island castle.

"For our new viewers, here's a quick recap," the commentator explained. "This is BattleScarz, a seven-minute deathmatch where two teams of five avatars compete to score the most kills. Each kill earns one point, with eliminated avatars respawning back into the game until the timer runs out. The team with the most points wins."

Wielding a sniper rifle, <Sahin> ascended the Topsie Tower, the game's highest vantage point and a perfect spot to overwatch and neutralize threats. <Arjan> took charge of the ground operations. <Eitan> and <Zafar> hunted in pairs while <Faiz> stayed close, ready to revive any fallen teammates.

<Arjan> approached the Choppy Chapel and scoped out its entrance, mindful of its reputation as a notorious camping spot. He lay in wait to intercept approaching enemies.

Elsewhere, <Eitan> and <Zafar> came under heavy fire. Crouched behind his mantlet shield, <Eitan> skillfully deflected a hail of bullets while <Zafar>, unfazed, continued scouring for hidden treasure chests.

"Are you serious, Zafar? I am under attack and you're busy looting," Eitan shouted into his microphone as enemy avatars closed in.

"Please hold them off a little longer, I'm almost done," Zafar responded over the comms.

"Are you serious?" Eitan's incredulous voice rang out.

Zafar fell silent, prompting Eitan's frustration to escalate. Desperate to buy some time, Eitan sought to disrupt his opponents' concentration as a last-ditch effort. With exaggerated theatrics, he bellowed into the public chat, "For the love of God, don't kill me! My wife and children need me! *Aaahhh!*" His voice rose to a shrill, ear-piercing wail.

"Focus, man!" Faiz interjected, though his attempt to sound serious was undercut by his own laughter at Eitan's hysterical shrieks echoing over the comms.

Just as <Eitan> was about to succumb, a rocket streaked over his shoulder, detonating amidst the enemies in a fiery explosion. Stunned, <Eitan> glanced back at <Zafar> as he struggled to catch his breath.

"Hey, drama queen, why don't you tell that to your imaginary family yourself?" Zafar quipped, his avatar winking playfully before discarding the spent RPG with a casual toss.

This game was a throwback to the Middle Ages with one striking twist. Instead of swords and arrows, the knights in shining armour wielded hyper-modern weaponry. From assault rifles to grenade launchers, the bleeding-edge armaments turned the mythical castle into a battlefield of unthinkable devastation. Ever wondered what medieval wars would look like with machine guns? This game brought that fantasy to virtual reality.

Returning to the game, the faint shuffle of enemy footsteps triggered Arjan's keen gamer ears, trained to pinpoint positions through sound. Anticipating their movement, he aimed at the open space and began counting under his breath. "3, 2…"

Boom!

He pre-fired, his instincts flawless as enemies walked straight into his line of fire. Meanwhile, <Sahin> picked off multiple foes with precise headshots.

The Aces may have drawn first blood, but Team Nucleus had their own aces up their sleeves. Led by their shrewd captain <Zoro>, Team Nucleus staged a swift comeback. Explosive traps near treasure chests lured <Eitan> and <Zafar> into a fatal blast and before <Faiz> could revive them, he was taken out by a gunner. With three Aces dead and <Arjan> stranded on the far side of the map, the opponents turned their gaze toward <Sahin>.

With no cover on the ground, <Sahin> was trapped atop the Topsie Tower. Two enemies crept stealthily toward the tower, evading his laser sights, while others kept him distracted with a fierce gun battle.

Decoding the pincer tactics, <Arjan> abandoned his cover and leapt into action. "Sahin, they're besieging the tower! Stay put, I am coming for you!" Arjan shouted through the comms as his avatar made a daring run for the tower.

Meanwhile, <Zoro> had already scaled the tower and snuck up on <Sahin>. With a soft tap on <Sahin>'s shoulder, <Zoro> caught him off guard. As <Sahin> turned, the enemy gently nudged him, throwing him off balance and sending him tumbling over the ledge to the jagged Deathly Rocks below.

The moment Faiz spectated <Arjan> sprinting defenceless across the open courtyard, he stood up from his chair in exasperation. He yelled into the mic, "What are you doing, Arjan? Sahin is dead, you cannot rescue…" Faiz's words were cut short as Arjan met a similar fate, swiftly taken down.

Zafar winced at Arjan's moment of brain fade. "C'mon, Arjan! That was a suicide mission. You were never going to save Sahin… but you could've at least saved yourself."

Eitan's tone was biting, "Bro's got a main character syndrome that he just can't shake off. EQ:1 IQ:0."

"Zip it!" Arjan snapped. "I wasn't being a hero. I couldn't just stand there and watch him get boxed in like that."

While the <Aces> waited to respawn, Team Nucleus added insult to injury, pulling out spray cans to deface Sahin's fallen avatar with graffiti of a tombstone.

The Aces seethed with rage at the disrespectful antics.

"They will regret this," Arjan murmured coldly, his grip tightening over the controller.

Team Nucleus seized the lead at 31:30 with only a minute remaining. The game was on a knife's edge. As the clock ticked down, Team Nucleus retreated into the shadows of the Dingy Dungeon.

"They're hiding like cowards," Arjan vented over the mic, annoyed by the evasive tactics.

"With the action shifting to the dungeon, Sahin's long-range skills become irrelevant. Could this be a masterstroke by Team Nucleus to sideline the world's best player in a critical moment?" the commentator speculated.

With no targets in sight, <Sahin> swapped his sniper for a close-range pistol and began descending the tower. Meanwhile, <Zafar> loaded a grenade launcher, ready to flush out the hiding enemies, while <Eitan> crafted the legendary Paladin's helmet, the game's most impenetrable armour, to bolster his defence. But the moment <Zafar>

and <Eitan> stepped into the Dingy Dungeon, they set off C4 explosives planted at the gates, reducing them to smithereens.

"The Aces have walked straight into a booby trap," the commentator exclaimed.

Team Nucleus stayed holed up in the Dingy Dungeon, further compounding the Aces' woes as they extended their lead to 33:30.

<Arjan> and <Faiz> crept forward, taking cover near the dungeon's main door. As they waited for the opportune moment, four enemies slipped out through secret passages while one stayed behind to keep them distracted. As the action unfolded, <Sahin> touched down and hurried toward the dungeon, desperate to join his teammates in a tense standoff. From a distance, Sahin caught sight of the escaped enemies circling around to mount an ambush on <Arjan> and <Faiz>, who remained oblivious to the impending danger.

In a dim, decrepit room, Sahin, clad in a black hoodie, pulled away from the game and frantically rummaged through a drawer. Amidst the clutter, Sahin found a dusty headset and hastily connected it to the console. "Look behind! Enemies are flanking you!" the high-pitched shriek, with its distinctly feminine timbre, reverberated through the comms.

Alerted by the heads-up, <Arjan> and <Faiz> spun around, catching the enemies off-guard, and eliminating three of them. The last flanking enemy, <Zoro>, made a desperate dash to flee, the score read '33-33' and the timer ticked down to the last 5 seconds… 4… 3… 2. In that moment, <Sahin> deftly pulled out a sniper and executed a no-scope headshot, taking down the fleeing enemy. The timer hit zero and the scoreboard lit up '34:33' in favour of the Squad Aces.

"Can you believe it? That headshot was a buzzer-beater. Aces have knocked Nucleus out of the tournament!" the commentator exclaimed, his voice filled with awe and disbelief.

As the celebrations unfurled, the Aces, miles apart from each other, reacted uniquely, yet in synchrony. Arjan slumped back in his gaming chair, shutting his eyes as a wave of relief washed over him.

Faiz whispered '*Takbir*', raising his hands in prayerful gratitude.

In stark contrast, Eitan's excitement bubbled over. He punched the air triumphantly, shouting, "Mazel tov!"

Meanwhile, Zafar exploded from his chair, dancing around the baby cot in hysterical glee and belting out gibberish tunes, *"Dum likka likka dum!"*

"Congratulations to the Squad Aces. They are now one step away from securing their spot in the WGC playoffs. Goodnight, and stay tuned for more exhilarating action!" the commentator signed off.

As the euphoria of victory settled, Arjan's eyes snapped open, a look of bewilderment stealing across his face. Scratching his head, he leaned into the microphone, "By the way, whose voice was that at the end? Sahin! Was that… you?" His voice faltered, disbelief creeping in.

A notification flashed on the screen: *Sahin has left the chat.*

"I think Sahin dropped off the conference," Faiz noted.

"It was Sahin, right?" Arjan pressed.

"Yes! Definitely him. Err… I mean her," Faiz stuttered.

"Oh my God!" Arjan's eyebrows shot up.

"Damn! Sahin is a girl? The world's best gamer is a girl. Can you believe that?" Eitan shook his head in disbelief.

"And I used to think that girls couldn't play. Wow!" Zafar confessed.

"Then consider this a sucker punch to your sexist face," Eitan chuckled.

"Shut up, noob!" Zafar hit back.

"Enough with the trash talk," Faiz interjected. "Do you guys realize if Sahin hadn't given us the heads-up, we'd have been toast?"

"Absolutely! You two were sitting ducks out there. Right, Arjan?" Eitan asked.

"She actually let her secret slip just to save us," Zafar acknowledged, a hint of respect in her voice.

"Arjan! Are you there?" Eitan asked.

An on-screen message popped up: *Arjan has left the chat.*

"There goes another one. Should I invite him back?" Eitan sighed.

"No, let him be," Faiz replied. "He's probably left the chat to talk to Sahin."

"Yup! They're pretty tight. This must've hit him harder," Zafar said.

"I just cannot wrap my head around the turn of events. What a night!" Eitan said.

"Phew!" Faiz let out a breath. "Let all of this sink in. See you guys tomorrow at the scrims."

Eitan chimed in, "Good game guys. Now, on to the next one. I can hardly wait."

With a fading tone, Zafar bid farewell. "Good game. Ciao."

As the chat window closed and the Aces logged off, Arjan paced restlessly in his room. The past twenty-four hours had been nothing short of a rollercoaster ride. He had journeyed through a spectrum of emotions, beginning with a crushing heartbreak, then soaring to the elation of a thrilling triumph, followed by the shock of a revelation, and even encountering a sting of betrayal in the mix that cut deeper considering the bond he shared with Sahin. Arjan felt a compelling urge to speak to Sahin, to unravel the tangled web of feelings that had gripped him. Taking a deep breath, he picked up his phone and voice called Sahin, ready to confront whatever – or rather, whoever – awaited him on the other end of the line.

4
Ready Player Two

The phone continued to ring, each beep winding the tension tighter in Arjan's chest. When the line finally connected, the silence that followed felt thicker than the wait. He rose from his gaming desk and walked over to the bed, perching on the edge. His mind scrambled for the right words to begin, but all that he managed to choke out was a hesitant 'Sahin'. The name spilled from his lips, wrapped in doubt and apprehension.

"Hi, Arjan," Sahin responded after a moment, her voice equally tentative.

The single word exchange only deepened the unease, freezing their conversation in its tracks. Arjan shifted uncomfortably, trying to shake the frost from his thoughts. He closed his eyes briefly, willing his thoughts into coherence.

He began again, his voice steadier but trembling under the weight of his words. "Remember last winter, when I was at my lowest? I still have the screenshot of what you wrote. It got me through nights when I felt like I was drowning. Your words kept me afloat. There were so many times I wanted to pick up the phone and say thank you. For your advice. For being there. For being you."

He faltered, his breath catching. "And now here we are. I don't even know who you are anymore. Suddenly, everything feels… false. I feel so blindsided."

His accusation lingered, sharp and cold. Sahin allowed it to settle, giving Arjan the space to vent.

He inhaled sharply, pushing himself forward. "This isn't about you being a man or a woman. What terrifies me is the thought that none of it was real. All this while. I've been living a lie, Sahin." He hesitated, his voice dropping to a near whisper. "If that's even your real name."

The words cut deep, but Sahin's voice, when it came, was measured. "Arjan, I understand how you feel, but I'm still the same person. Nothing has changed. With due respect, I think… you're overreacting. Our bond was never about gender or identities – it was about trust, connection, and everything we've shared."

Her words resonated, stirring something within him, but he remained guarded, his thoughts clouded.

"I don't know," he said, his voice low. "How am I supposed to believe that? How do I know this isn't just another half-truth?"

"I get it," she said gently. "You're angry. Hurt. But I swear – everything that mattered, everything I said, everything I felt – it was real. There were no lies."

Her calmness began to soften the edges of Arjan's anger. The more he listened, the more her words settled over him like a balm, even as doubts still churned in his mind.

He exhaled sharply. "Then why didn't you tell me? Why keep it a secret?"

Sahin hesitated before answering. "It wasn't about trust, Arjan. It was survival." She paused, her voice quieter now. "I wanted to tell you, but I couldn't. Girls here aren't allowed to interact with strangers – it's a complete taboo. If my father found out… he wouldn't just destroy my PlayStation… he would destroy everything."

The weight of her vulnerability hit him like a wave, washing away the anger he'd been holding onto. "Oh… that bad? Where are you from?" he asked.

"Rojava," she replied.

"Where's that?"

Her lips curled into a wry smile. "Never mind. We don't expect outsiders to know." Her sarcasm was sharp, but not unkind. "Anyway! Look at the bright side. The fact that you didn't know I was a girl is what made our friendship so innocent."

Arjan shrugged, his tone lightening. "I am not sure about that. For what it's worth, desperate guys falling for fake women's Facebook profiles don't know the real gender on the other end either. So much for innocence!"

Sahin blinked, then burst into laughter. "Wow, that's your big takeaway from all this?"

His joke might have been lame, but it managed to immediately dissolve the tension that had weighed so heavily, restoring the easy connection that had always been there.

"Okay, tell me, what difference would it have made if you'd known I was a girl? Would you have treated me any differently?"

"Off the top of my head," Arjan said, a half-smile forming. "I probably wouldn't have kept calling you 'bro' all the time."

"Pfft! Don't worry about that, brooo!" Sahin teased, drawing out the word just to rub it in.

"Yeah, sure. Keep at it, to your heart's content."

"Maybe you would've even flirted with me," Sahin ventured.

"Oh! Really? What makes you say that?" Arjan asked.

"You're from Delhi, right?" Sahin said, a knowing tone in her voice.

Arjan felt the jab and quickly wanted to steer away. "Damn! Are Delhi boys that notorious? Anyway, whatever… I'll let that slide."

His words came out in a rush, almost tripping over themselves as he hurried to change the subject. "What else? Are you working or still studying?"

"A little bit of both," Sahin said. "I'm trying to get into the architecture programme at Ankara University."

"Ah, Turkey. That's cool," Arjan said, already stroking his chin as if thinking about his next question. "What else can I ask you?"

"Hold on a second," Sahin interjected. "Why do you get to ask all the questions?"

"Because my life's an open book, but you're the one who's kept your identity so tightly under wraps," Arjan shot back with a smirk.

"I rest my case," Sahin said dryly. "I can't help but wonder if this sudden flood of curiosity has anything to do with the fact that you know I'm a girl now?"

Arjan stumbled for a response, momentarily tongue-tied. "I'm just naturally curious, that's all," he mumbled. Then his eyebrows puckered as a thought struck him. "Wait a minute! Now that we're nearly through to the playoffs, wouldn't you have to drop your incognito act anyway?"

"Well, it has been playing on my mind," Sahin admitted. "But I keep thinking that I'll cross that bridge when I come to it."

Arjan nodded slowly. "Hmm, I hope you weren't planning on ghosting us on the big stage. That would totally blow."

Sahin took a moment to reply, "Come on, you know I wouldn't do that… or would I?" she added with a teasing note, trying to deflect the seriousness. "Besides, we still have one more game to win, remember? Let's not get ahead of ourselves."

Arjan forced a chuckle, not entirely convinced by the playful tone. "Fair enough. Anyway, great game today. You always find a way to save me."

"Thanks! Have you heard Shahrukh Khan's famous dialogue in the movie *Veer Zaara*?" Sahin asked.

"You know Shahrukh Khan?" Arjan's surprise was evident.

"Do you think I live under a rock or something?"

"Of course not, but this? You could've told me sooner."

"It never came up. Anyway… I'm a big fan. He's very popular in my country. Born on 2nd November, he hails from the same city as you. See I know that too. No one pulls off onscreen romance quite like he does."

Arjan raised an eyebrow, starting to catch on. "So that's where you got the notion about Delhi boys being hopeless romantics, huh?"

"Obviously! What did you think?"

"Uh, never mind."

"So, I was saying – in that movie, the actress, Pretty Zinda, I think?"

"Preity Zinta. Go on…"

"She asks Shahrukh, 'How many times are you going to rescue me?' And he replies in his trademark style…" Sahin paused for dramatic effect, then delivered the line in broken but earnest Hindi, *"Tum jitni baar apni jaan gavaaogi, Zaara."* She hesitated for a second, then added, "Which, I think, means something like, 'Every time you risk your life, I'll be there to save you.'"

Arjan chuckled, appreciating her effort. "Yeah, that's pretty close. But what are you trying to say?"

"Duh! It's the same with us, Arjan! I've literally lost count of the times I've rescued you in the game. Every time you're in trouble; I appear to save you!"

"Very funny," Arjan said, rolling his eyes but smiling. "By the way, you speak such fluent Hindi."

"Don't make fun of my Hindi," Sahin replied playfully.

Sensing the shift, Sahin said, "By the way, you call me your life coach and all, but maybe if you actually followed my advice about relationships, you wouldn't have kept walking straight into one red flag after another."

A small, sheepish smile pulled at Arjan's lips. "Guilty as charged," he admitted. "Bad luck with girls or maybe I haven't found the perfect one! I've been burning my fingers all the time."

Sahin chuckled softly. "It's okay. I'll patch you up. Hope always."

★ ★ ★

Arjan lounged on a recliner, staring out the window, his thoughts drifting. The TV droned in the background: "More than a million Iraqis have fled their homes as ISIS continues its armed siege…"

Something snapped him back to reality. With a slight wince, he turned to the TV, grabbed the remote, and began flicking through channels. He paused on *Saving Private Ryan*, just as the gripping climax unfolded. Tom Hanks, battered and bloodied, sat propped against a motorcycle, staring down a German Tiger tank rumbling closer, crushing a sandbag bunker beneath its treads. Arjan sat up slightly, drawn into the action. Hanks drew his handgun and fired; the shots futile against the advancing tank – until it suddenly erupted in flames. Hanks looked up in disbelief as a fighter jet roared overhead.

Inspired, Arjan sprang to his feet and grabbed his Nerf gun. His softly-lit bedroom became a battlefield. Stealthily, he crept behind the recliner, his gaze locking on the enemy: a five-inch Darth Vader figurine perched on the bookshelf. He cocked the slider, took a deep breath and fired. The foam dart zipped through the air, striking Darth Vader, sending it tumbling to the floor. Triumphant, he pumped his fist, grinning at his flawless aim, when a message pinged. Glancing around, he scanned the cluttered room for his phone. He quickly muted the TV, as humans have come to agree, turning down the volume somehow sharpens vision. The echoes of battle faded into silence as he switched on the lights. His eyes landed on his phone near the edge of the bed. The screen flashed: *PlayStation App: Sahin is online now.*

He'd seen this notification countless times before, but tonight it landed differently. A flush crept up his cheeks, and his breath hitched for a moment. Grabbing the controller, he powered on his gaming rig. Never before had the PlayStation startup come with this strange, fluttering anticipation. Not even the most intense boss fights had made his pulse race like this. Gaming suddenly felt charged with an extra spark that he couldn't quite define. He wasn't just logging on to play anymore. He was logging on for her.

A few days later, Arjan sat slouched in the middle row of the lecture hall, half-listening as the professor, a balding man in his fifties, droned on about ethics in journalism. The lecture blended into a monotonous hum, and Arjan's mind began to wander, far from the dusty blackboard and half-filled notebooks surrounding him.

His phone buzzed in his pocket. With a furtive glance, he slid it out and unlocked the screen.

Sahin: *Hi Arjan. Aren't we supposed to be playing right now?*

A blush spread across Arjan's cheeks as he typed.

Arjan: *Stuck in the lecture hall. Can't wait to join you.*

Across the room, Priya noticed, her eyes narrowing with quiet jealousy as she sulked at his love-struck expression.

Sahin: *Come soon, I'll be waiting.*

Arjan: *On my wa—*

Ouch!

Before he could finish his reply, a piece of chalk sailed through the air, hitting him squarely on the forehead. The class burst into laughter as Arjan rubbed the sore spot.

The professor, furious, pointed a stern finger at him. "No phones in class! How many times do I need to tell you, you disobedient brats?"

The moment passed, but Arjan's grin lingered, Sahin's words echoing in his mind.

Arjan and Sahin had always been close, but the revelation of her identity had shifted everything. It opened a whole new dimension to their relationship, sparking conversations that stripped away layers of formality, exposing a vulnerability that was both exciting and uncharted. Suddenly, no topic felt off-limits. Whether they were at home, running errands, or sitting through dull lectures, their conversations flowed endlessly. Neither of them knew where this was heading, but one thing was clear: things between them would never be the same. Their connection deepened fast. What began as casual banter evolved into meaningful exchanges, and voice calls naturally turned into video chats. It was funny, really, how much the dynamics had shifted – he found himself second-guessing his words, hyper-aware of how he looked, things he'd never worried about when she was just 'one of the guys'.

The other night, Arjan stood at the bathroom mirror, carefully shaving his stubble. He rifled through his wardrobe, tossing shirts onto the bed until he settled on a trendy dress shirt. A quick dab of styling gel tamed his hair, and a few spritzes of cologne filled the room with a sharp scent. As he admired his reflection, his mother stopped at the half-open door. Wrinkling her nose at the overpowering scent, she asked, "Where are you off to at this hour? It's so late."

"Mummy, I'm not going anywhere," Arjan replied, trying to sound casual.

"Then why are you so decked up?" she teased, her eyes narrowing.

"Just like that," he mumbled, suddenly self-conscious.

"Dressing up at midnight 'just like that'? *Tujhe vakhri jawaani chaddhi hai. So jaa!*"

"Mom, please!" he groaned, shutting the door as her laughter faded down the hall.

His phone buzzed with a video-call notification from Sahin. His breath hitched, and his fingers fumbled slightly as he tapped to answer. The screen flickered to life, and there she was. Sahin, sitting in a dimly lit room, lifted the hood over her head, revealing her disarmingly beautiful face. The brilliant radiance on her face lit up the whole screen. Arjan stared, unblinkingly, spellbound by her presence. She was fair to a fault, with captivating gray eyes that seemed to pull him into their depths. She casually brushed the strands of her flowing brown mane away from her face. "Hi Arjan," she greeted softly, her lips curving into a gentle smile.

He blinked, startled out of his trance. "Hey, Sahin," he managed, his voice shakier than he'd hoped.

Sahin giggled lightly.

Arjan's nerves slowly settled, but clearly, this was no longer just a friendship. Something deeper had begun to bloom between them, and it was thrilling, even if a little terrifying. They may have come from worlds apart, but their connection felt far stronger than any distance.

A few days later, as Arjan sprawled on his bed, he held the ornate frame in his hands, now holding the photo of him and Sahin – a goofy screenshot from one of their video calls. The frame had found its way back to his room, thanks to his mother, who clearly thought it too good to discard, despite the scars it bore from its flight into the trash.

With Sahin's photo nestled inside, the frame seemed reborn, much like Kintsugi, its imperfections only adding to the charm. But it wasn't just the frame that had been restored. Sahin had mended him too, her gold weaving through his cracks, making his life feel far more beautiful than he'd ever imagined.

Just as her thoughts lingered in his mind, his phone buzzed. Without even glancing at the screen, Arjan answered. "Hello?"

"*Pyaar dosti hai,*" Sahin began abruptly, skipping any preamble.

"What? Do you really mean that?" Arjan asked, thrown off by the sudden declaration.

"I've been practicing that line for the last twenty minutes… well, I truly do," she said a little softly.

"Ah! So that's why no hi, no hello! You had to spit it out before losing the flow!" Arjan teased as his cheeks flushed.

"Well, it's a classic, and I wanted to nail the delivery," Sahin shot back with a smile.

"It's super cheesy even for Bollywood," Arjan chuckled, shaking his head.

"Alright then," she countered with a playful challenge. "Your turn. Impress me."

Arjan paused thoughtfully. "Hmm, I've got one from your favourite movie."

"*Veer Zaara?*" she guessed, her curiosity piqued. "Bring it on."

He cleared his throat theatrically. "*Agar tumhe kabhi dost ki zarurat pade, toh bas itna yaad rakhna ki sarhad paar ek aisa shaks hai jo aapke liye apni jaan bhi de dega.* It means…"

"Arjan," Sahin interrupted, her tone half-teasing, half-serious. "Duh! I know what it means. The real question is: do you mean it?"

"Of course!" Arjan said. "I may not exactly be *sarhad paar*, but this *shaks* would still go to the ends of the earth for you. I really mean it."

"Uh-huh," she said, laughing. "And now, who's the cheesy one?"

And just like that, their friendship transformed into something much more. They talked for hours, losing all sense of time. Somewhere between their endless phone calls and late-night gaming sessions, they had fallen for each other – truly, madly, deeply. It wasn't a sudden realization, but rather a quiet, undeniable feeling that had grown between them, until it consumed them both without either of them noticing when or how it started. And with a sprinkle of SRK's brand of romance, their relationship seemed to mirror the kind of magic only found in the movies they both adored.

In the virtual arena, <Arjan> and <Sahin> walked hand in hand, oblivious to the surroundings while their teammates <Eitan>, <Zafar> and <Faiz> fought the enemy team in a scrim game.

Eitan, pinned down under heavy fire, shouted into the party chat, frustration rising in his voice, "Hello! We could really use some backup fire here!"

But Arjan and Sahin were far from the battle in their minds. They did not deign to respond to the rescue call as their avatars remained locked in each other's gaze.

Faiz, seeing their lack of response, scoffed. "What's wrong with these two? Get a room, lovebirds!"

Ignoring the taunts, <Arjan> leaned in and planted a kiss on <Sahin>'s right cheek in the middle of the digital warzone. The incongruity of romance amid gunfire made the moment feel even more surreal. Somewhere between the pixels and the real world, a torrid love affair was blossoming. An in-game notification widget popped up in the corner of the screen. *Achievement Unlocked: Love knows no boundaries.*

5
Kamikaze Glitch

The final qualifier was upon them. Squad Aces and their opponents, distinguished by blue and red mantlings on their gothic armour suits, were ferried toward the imposing Halcyon Castle. Both teams radiated a quiet focus as they steeled themselves for the ultimate clash.

In his room, Arjan was a bundle of nerves, rocking in his chair as he focused on the glowing screen. The pressure was immense – one bad game could unravel a year's worth of preparations and crush his dreams. This was more than just a game. It was a golden opportunity to meet his squad mates in person, especially Sahin, and prove to himself, and his father, that his passion was a valid career path, not a waste of time. An early exit wouldn't just sting – it could drive him to seriously question everything he'd worked for. Arjan knew he needed this victory, not just to advance, but to quell doubts and prove he was right to follow his heart against all odds.

As the countdown began, Arjan spritzed his nasal spray – a ritual etched into his pre-game routine. Clearing his throat, he turned on his mic. "Good luck, everyone!" His voice wavered, betraying a tremor of doubt.

"Yeah! Let's wreck 'em!" Zafar roared.

"We've got this, team!" Sahin chimed in, sounding pumped.

"It's our time to shine," Faiz declared.

Silence followed, where Eitan's voice should have been.

"Eitan, you there?" Arjan asked, unease creeping in as the silence stretched too close to the match's start.

"Eitan! Not the best time to pull a Houdini, man," Faiz warned, half-exasperated.

Just then, the jarring noise of a toilet flushing blared through their headsets. As much as the mental image of Eitan mid-bathroom break vividly assaulted their senses, the team was relieved to know Eitan was still connected, even if his microphone was picking up rather unfortunate sounds.

As Eitan scrambled to adjust his headset, the rustling audible, Faiz couldn't help but remark, "Seriously, dude? Seconds away from the biggest match of our lives and you're… taking a dump?"

"Oh no, was my mic on? That's embarrassing," Eitan finally blurted out, his voice a sheepish squeak. "Sorry, guys. Just dealing with some intense match-day jitters."

A burst of genuine laughter rolled through the team, the absurdity of the situation melting away their pre-game nerves.

"Did anyone catch the sound of the sink, or was it just that epic flush?" Zafar quipped.

Sahin joined in the banter. "Just don't touch the controller with those grimy hands."

"Too late for that," Eitan chuckled.

"Eww," Sahin uttered in feigned horror.

The laughter swelled.

Arjan chuckled before reeling them back in. "Alright, enough. Focus guys."

The commentator's voice boomed, setting the stage. "It's Squad Aces versus Cyber Chaos, an all-Russian powerhouse, in the final qualifier. A win leads to glory in Munich; a loss leads to nowhere."

As the Viking ships docked, the Aces stormed ashore, all guns blazing. <Arjan> and <Eitan> led the offensive, mowing down enemies. <Zafar> hurled grenades, flushing the enemies out into the open, while Sahin, stationed atop the Topsie Tower, picked them off with her trusty sniper rifle.

"Good work, team. Let's go for the kill," Arjan said, beaming at the dominant scoreline.

In an aggressive move, <Sahin> descended the tower and joined the Aces on the ground. <Eitan> spotted an enemy avatar on the drawbridge. Before he could get a shot off, the enemy vanished into thin air. Moments later, the enemy reappeared, charging from the opposite end. <Eitan> held his nerve and fired point-blank, taking the enemy down. Relief turned to horror as a cluster grenade fell from the enemy's hand.

BOOM!

The grenade erupted into multiple blasts, devastating the entire Aces squad within its deadly radius.

"Woah! That is a squad wipe. With one sacrifice, the Cybers have racked up five precious kills," the commentator announced.

The smile vanished from Arjan's face as he squinted at the screen in disbelief.

"Let's regroup and refocus," Arjan said, rallying the team. "Back to basics, spread out and deny them squad-kills."

Upon respawning, <Sahin> ascended the Topsie Tower, locked onto a charging enemy and took aim. Just as her shot was about to connect, the enemy glitched and teleported out of danger. "Oh God! They are using a speed glitch," she alerted, rolling her eyes in frustration.

Like a battering ram, the glitching enemy burst into the Choppy Chapel and detonated on impact. Four Aces were obliterated as the chapel went up in flames. The scoreboard flashed: Aces: 14, Cybers: 15.

"Cyber Chaos has surged ahead. Unsporting exploits or not, they are reaping the rewards. As they say, all's fair in love and war," the commentator remarked.

"Exploits? These cyber cowards are downright cheating. They are using the Kamikaze glitch," Sahin fumed.

"*Kaun Qazi*? (Kamikaze who?) What sorcery is that?" Zafar asked.

The term 'Kamikaze' surfaced during the fag-end of World War II, when Japan, facing inevitable defeat, resorted to desperate measures. Kamikaze were airmen turned suicide bombers who deliberately crashed their improvised planes into Allied Warships in a last-ditch effort, leaving the bloodiest imprint on the Pacific Theatre. Named after this historical phenomenon, the Kamikaze glitch in video games combines two lethal hacks. The speed hack renders a momentary sprint burst while the explosion hack creates a massive explosion upon death that kills all opponents in its blast radius.

Using this nefarious tactic, Cyber Chaos was sending avatar after avatar to ram into Squad Aces and blow them on the cheap. Meanwhile, another avatar dodged <Sahin>'s sniper fire and bombed the hapless Aces on the ground.

"Do not go anywhere. The prodigious Cyber Chaos have mounted a stunning comeback," the commentator exclaimed.

Arjan stared at the replay. "This is so not fair. How are they getting away with this?" he muttered, clutching the gaming controller so tightly he could crush it.

"They've bypassed every hacking checkpoint. They're packing some serious tech," Faiz speculated, his tone grim.

"What's wrong with the commentator and officials? Can't anyone see they're cheating?" Eitan ranted, echoing team's shared frustration.

"I'm afraid they're masking their hacks too well. To an untrained eye, it would appear nothing more than an innocuous glitch," Faiz explained, his voice resigned.

"Come on, we've got to do something. Can't we report them?" Eitan whined.

"They may be cheating but we still have to beat them to stay in the competition. If they've gotten this far without being flagged, I doubt anything will change now," Faiz reasoned.

"But…" Eitan protested weakly.

The Aces respawned, only to be zapped by a hail of explosions. The floor was literally lava. Every tactic failed. Flanking maneuvers were cut down instantly. An ambush near the Regal Cathedral went horribly wrong, with the Aces wiped out in a blink. Desperation grew as Arjan rigged Wooden Keep's entrance with proximity mines, hoping to trigger the kamikazes prematurely. But the Cybers speed-glitched over the trap, swarming the Aces effortlessly. The Cyber bots ran amok, widening their lead to 31:15.

Arjan tore off his headset and flung his controller aside. Dropping his head into his hands, he muttered, "This can't be how it ends. The championship, meeting Sahin – it can't all be ruined by a bunch of cheats. I refuse to accept this!"

Sensing his distress, Mario pounced onto his lap, licking his face in an attempt to comfort him. Arjan resisted at first, then gently shooed him away. Mario, understanding, climbed down but stayed close, watching his master intently.

After a pause, Arjan's eyes snapped open, resolve replacing despair. He sat upright, slipping his headset back on. "Doc! Are you there?" he called, his voice steadier. As if on cue, Mario retrieved the discarded controller, dropping it at Arjan's feet like a loyal sidekick.

"I don't rage-quit," Faiz replied, though his tone was deflated.

"Can you rig the mines?" Arjan asked urgently.

"What do you mean?"

"Can you tweak the trip mine's fuse timer to detonate instantly at the slightest movement?"

"Arjan! I've told you already – they have sophisticated tech. They can mask their moves. Ours isn't nearly as advanced."

"So what?" Arjan shot back. "We are going to be kicked out anyway if those suicide bots keep swarming us like fucking homing missiles. We're sitting ducks."

"I'm an ethical hacker. Cheating is haram. My conscience won't allow it," Faiz stated firmly.

"Get off your high horse, Mr Prude," Eitan scoffed, unable to contain his disgruntlement.

"Shut it, Eitan!" Faiz snarled.

"Are you seriously okay with letting those cheats walk away with this?" Arjan ventured, his voice tense.

"Come on, Faiz! Our faith also teaches us to stand for what's right," Zafar implored, his voice earnest as he sought to sway Faiz.

"Yes, and we are in the right here; those cheats are in the wrong. We must not let evil triumph over good. It is our moral duty—" Arjan began, his voice swelling.

Faiz cut him off, "Arjan! Enough, kill the theatrics." He sighed deeply, grappling with the decision before him. After a moment of reflection, he whispered a religious verse, *"Astaghfirullah wa atubu ilaih,"* seeking forgiveness for what he was about to do. Turning back to the microphone, he added, "I'll try. Don't expect miracles – I've never tampered with the mines before."

"No pressure, Doc," Arjan said encouragingly.

"Will Squad Aces hold, or will Cyber Chaos pull off a miraculous comeback? We're in the final moments of this epic battle!" the commentator declared.

The Aces waited, tension palpable, as their rigged trip mines lay in wait at the Lords' Hall. Faiz leaned in; palms pressed together. "Please trip. Please trip!" he whispered.

Arjan, hands clasped in prayerful hope, softly recited, *"Jai Hanuman Gyan Gun Sagar…"* while Eitan muttered a Hebrew verse, their eyes glued to the screen.

"Hope always," Sahin murmured, her voice tinged with quiet optimism.

The Kamikazes surged forward, sprint-glitching to evade the mines. But Faiz's tweaks worked. The hypersensitive mines erupted, blowing up two enemies in a fiery blast. The remaining Kamikazes faltered, scrambling to retreat, only to be picked off by <Sahin>'s deadly sniper.

"*Takbir.* It works!" Faiz exclaimed, leaning back with a relieved sigh.

"You're the doc, Doc!" Arjan cheered.

"*Jab hum ne maar li hai baazi, toh kya karega (Kami)Qazi,*" Zafar quipped, chuckling as the sole fan of his wordplay.

Another wave of Kamikazes rushed the Squire's Spire but met their end as a hypersensitive mine exploded on impact.

Faiz's fingers flew over his keyboard, tirelessly crunching the codes.

"This works like a charm. Arjan, you're a genius!" Sahin gushed.

"Thanks, love," Arjan grinned, blowing an exaggerated kiss.

"Really? I'm pulling this hack off and you're running away with the credit?" Faiz interjected.

"This idea was my brainchild after all," Arjan quipped, clearly enjoying the banter.

"Fine, you babysit your brainchild while I take a bio break," Faiz shot back.

"Hey, hey! Relax, I got carried away. I trust you with my child, Doc," Arjan said.

"Always extra, aren't you?" Faiz muttered with a chuckle.

The battlefield fell eerily quiet. The Kamikazes, instead of their usual chaotic charge, stopped in their tracks.

"This is weird. Is their hack crashing?" Zafar ventured, his voice tinged with cautious hope.

Faiz analyzed the backend, his expression grim. "This isn't a bug. It's deliberate. They're up to something."

Unease gripped the Aces as the Kamikazes began moving again – but this time with chilling precision. One by one, they formed a single-file line like soldiers marching into battle.

Then, as if on cue, the line surged forward, a deadly cascade of bombers poised to wreak havoc.

"They've found a loophole!" Faiz exclaimed, his voice rising. "The mines won't take them all out. They'll handle the first one, maybe two, but the cooldown is too long to stop the rest."

"Oh my God!" the Aces exclaimed in unison.

As feared, the first Kamikaze martyred itself, falling flat onto the mines and neutralizing the entire minefield. Four kamikazes, still at large, capered over the dead mines and breached the Aces' positions.

"We're on our own now. Brace yourselves!" Eitan shrieked. Panic spread among the Aces as they prepared to face the killer wave meant to wipe them out in one fell swoop.

"Space out, everyone. Another squad kill means instant defeat," Arjan commanded.

"Oh God, what now? Fight or flight?" Eitan choked out, his heart pounding.

"Both," Arjan said firmly. "It's our only shot."

"Both? What do you mean?" Eitan asked, bewildered.

"Keep your distance and aim for their heads," Arjan explained. "Think of it like killing creepers in Minecraft."

"They are speed glitching, remember? Forget headshots, they are too fast even for body shots," Zafar pointed out the obvious challenge.

"Do we have any other choice?" Arjan snapped, his patience wearing thin.

<Eitan> equipped the legendary Paladin's helmet. "I've got a better plan. I'll charge at them and blow myself up before they reach us. Trust me, they won't see it coming," he declared as his avatar recklessly bolted forward.

"Hey! Wrong direction, genius!" Sahin yelled.

In utter confusion, <Eitan> tripped over and met a quick, lonely death.

"Goddammit!" Faiz groaned.

"You were right – no one actually saw you coming," Zafar quipped, unable to resist the jab even in the grim situation.

Rubbing salt in the wound, the enemy captain, Vlad sauntered over and looted the Paladin's helmet from Eitan's lifeless avatar.

"My bad. Vlad even took my helmet," Eitan admitted sheepishly.

"Argh! Don't tell me, Eitan. With that helmet, it is going to be even harder to take them down," Sahin lamented, her anxiety spiking.

"Arjan, incoming!" Faiz suddenly cried out, spotting an imminent threat.

As <Vlad> charged at <Arjan>, the latter dodge-rolled and fired. The bullet ricocheted off the fully armored Paladin's helmet, but its impact stun-locked <Vlad>.

Sensing an opportunity to disarm him, <Zafar> and <Faiz> rushed toward him and grappled him around the neck. Just as <Arjan> prepared to deliver a knockout blow, a flashbang exploded, disorienting the Aces. In the chaos, <Vlad> slipped away. Before the Aces could recover, sniper shots rang out, eliminating them.

The score flashed, "Cybers:34, Aces:31." All Aces were down except for <Sahin>.

With four enemies hot on her heels, <Sahin> made a daring run for it. While she kited the enemies, she deftly dropped a mine in her wake. Two of the enemies, too caught up in the chase, triggered the tweaked mine. It detonated with a sharp crack, like mosquitoes meeting an electric swatter, instantly zapping them both.

Seizing the moment, <Sahin> spun around and caught another enemy off guard, taking him down before he could glitch to safety. With three adversaries down, the odds quickly evened to a one-on-one. Realizing the Cybers were playing into Sahin's hands, <Vlad> the last standing kamikaze, vanished like a ghost. <Sahin> looked around cluelessly.

"Keep your head on a swivel. He'll strike when you least expect it," Faiz warned.

"What do I do now?" Sahin asked her spectating teammates, her voice taut with tension.

"That helmet is headshot proof," Arjan groused.

"Exactly! No chink in that armour," Eitan said, as if marveling at his own handiwork.

"What a time to brag, especially after you gift-wrapped it for Vlad," Arjan shot back.

"Prepare for the worst!" Zafar lamented, his tone defeatist.

Just then, <Vlad> reappeared from the edge of the curtain wall, sprint-glitching straight at <Sahin>. Sahin quickly spotted him but didn't flinch. Steadying her breath, she trained her sniper's reticle on the helmet's ocularium. As she pulled the trigger, she swayed the weapon just enough to compensate for the avatar's rapid trajectory. *BAM!* The bullet sliced cleanly through the helmet's narrow eye-slits, killing <Vlad> instantly.

"Woah! How did she squeeze a bullet through that visor?" Eitan popped off his chair in a stupor.

But the game was not won yet. Before perishing, Vlad had gotten close enough to keep Sahin within the blast radius. His dead avatar could detonate any moment. Thinking fast, Sahin unloaded a barrage of shots, each bullet knocking the corpse back toward the curtain wall. As it teetered on the edge, <Sahin> delivered the coup de grace that sent it flying off the ledge. BOOM! Vlad's remains exploded mid-air, the castellations shattering, but Sahin was out of harm's way. The Aces won the match with a spectacular finish.

"Sahin's on a tear! With a string of clutches, he's carried the team to victory," the commentator roared. "If anything, today's performance will only flare up the media buzz around Sahin's first-ever public appearance in Munich. Mind you, the reclusive phenom, has stayed anonymous despite bursting onto the gaming scene back in 2012."

In jubilation, the Aces huddled together in the virtual arena. The commentator signed off with a flourish, "Congratulations to Squad Aces on a resounding victory. That's all for now. See you soon in Germany."

Arjan broke into frenzied dance moves, with Mario prancing excitedly around him.

"We did it guys! We've qualified for the world's biggest championship," Faiz exclaimed, his voice brimming with pride.

"We are just one step away from winning that coveted trophy," Zafar added.

"All hail Sahin! What a player," Arjan cheered.

"The hoopla around Sahin's big reveal is getting crazier. Imagine how it'll explode when everyone learns that the world number one is a girl," Faiz pondered aloud.

"To be honest, I am low-key jealous. It is our first major land tournament as well, yet nobody is talking about us," Eitan said.

"I'll tell you why," Faiz began, "Could you have landed a headshot through those tiny eyeholes like she did?" He paused for emphasis, then added, "Especially with Vlad glitching?"

Eitan was left speechless.

"I'd have loved to have a crack at that. It just never crossed my mind to aim like that," Arjan said thoughtfully.

"Oh, come on Arjan! You know that was a one-in-a-million shot," Faiz countered. "Sahin's the GOAT."

Suddenly, an on-screen message appeared – *Sahin left the voice chat*.

"Where did she go now?" Zafar asked.

"She's probably drained from carrying us to victory. Let her rest," Faiz suggested.

"The overwhelming hype around her first appearance has been taking a toll on her lately," Arjan said.

"Why? Did she say something?" Zafar inquired.

"Her family's very orthodox. They don't even know about her gaming stint," Arjan revealed.

"Really? Then how is she going to travel to Germany with all those restrictions?" Eitan asked, concerned.

"She said she'll figure something out. I'm sure she will," Arjan reassured.

"Guys! If there's anything you should be worrying about, it's packing your bags for Munich," Faiz interjected.

"I can't wait to see you all. I'm so stoked right now! We did it, guys," Arjan said.

"Woohoo! Munich, here we come," Eitan cheered.

"Wait a minute. Don't you already live there?" Arjan asked, raising an eyebrow.

"Yeah, like twenty minutes away. But saying it like that hits different," Eitan joked.

"Ah! Long distance," Arjan teased with a grin.

With a parting laugh, Faiz said, "See you soon, guys!"

As the Aces wrapped up a thrilling session amidst laughter and banter, their excitement was palpable. This moment was unlike any before; it felt like the prelude to something far greater. As their virtual avatars faded from the game lobby, they left behind a promise: their next gathering would be face-to-face in Munich. Eager to transform their online triumphs into tangible glory, they were ready to step out from the shadows of their digital personas and prove themselves as champions on the world stage, not just in pixels but also in flesh and blood.

6
Beyond Virtual Reality

For years, Arjan had harbored dreams of reaching the pinnacle in competitive gaming, often fearing that a single misstep could dwindle his fiery passion to a mere hobby. His squad's recent victory had put them on the map – a triumph of grand slam proportions. Naturally, he was on cloud nine, armed with a solid gold proof to show for his efforts, shutting down every doubt about the hours he'd poured into video games. Yet, amidst the celebration, the anticipation of meeting Sahin in person for the first time overshadowed everything.

In the days leading up to departure for Munich, Arjan threw himself into a whirlwind of preparations that could make a bridezilla look complacent. Each day was a countdown, every move a step closer to the moment. He wasn't just preparing; he was leveling up the avatar he wished to present to Sahin, beyond the code and game chats. With a fresh haircut, he launched into a shopping spree worthy of Fashion Week. Sifting through racks of designer threads, he picked out several high-end ensembles – splurging like a pre-teen gamer dropping virtual cash on premium skins.

Having checked off the side quests of personal vanity, Arjan turned his focus to the story mission. His hunt for the perfect proposal ring led him to a quaint jewellery shop. He sought a stone that would eloquently convey his feelings, neither whispering empty promises nor shouting bold declarations. It had to strike the right balance: not desperate, yet not too casual. After much deliberation, he chose a dainty diamond ring. His online search for an ideal proposal venue ended at a Michelin-starred restaurant in the historic Marienplatz for its dreamy ambiance. He meticulously planned the evening, arranging a candlelit table at the restaurant, curating a bespoke menu, and selecting the finest champagne – all to create an unforgettable experience. Adding a personal flourish, he organized for a band to serenade them with their cherished romantic Bollywood melodies.

With the ring in hand and the restaurant's 'deluxe proposal package' booked, it was now time to master the charm that would sweep Sahin off her feet. He rehearsed his proposal in front of the bedroom mirror, channeling his inner Shahrukh Khan. Dropping to one knee, he extended his hand, ring glinting softly. "Will you marry me?" he practiced, hoping to evoke just a fraction of SRK's magic. With each repetition, his confidence swelled, and his delivery became smoother, yet the butterflies in his stomach refused to settle.

As the day of departure arrived, Rajesh and Anita stood beside him at the airport, their expressions soft as he unloaded his luggage from the car.

"Have a safe flight. Call us as soon as you land." Anita's words enveloped him in a warm embrace.

Arjan nodded and turned to his father. A quiet moment passed as he bowed to touch Rajesh's feet, seeking his blessings.

"Cannot wait for you to win the cup and prove your father wrong," Anita added, her tone teasing.

Arjan's eyebrows puckered in disbelief, his look one of confused exasperation, questioning her choice of moment to stir the pot. Eager to avoid a potential crossfire, he quickly turned his attention to his luggage.

After a brief pause, Rajesh said, "And your mother knows that no one would be happier than me to be proven wrong."

The unexpected vulnerability in his words left them speechless.

"Win or lose, it's your belief in your passion that makes us very proud," Rajesh added, his tone warm as he opened his arms for a hug.

"Papa, hearing this from you... it means everything to me," Arjan replied, his voice thick with emotion as he stepped into his father's embrace.

While the father and son shared the heartfelt moment, Anita, ever ready with a gentle tease, quipped, "Well, that's quite the change of heart."

"Nah! I'm just being diplomatic. Once this video-game fever dies down, he'll come running back to the family business," Rajesh quipped.

The remark drew a light-hearted laugh, easing the emotional moment.

Buoyed by his parents' love and support, Arjan headed to the gate with a genuine smile on his face. The championship no longer felt daunting; it was now a journey he was ready to enjoy, knowing he'd already won where it mattered most.

* * *

Nine hours into its journey, an Air India Boeing jet made a graceful descent onto the tarmac of Munich Airport, marking the beginning of a much-awaited chapter in Arjan's life. As another hour ticked by, he stepped into a bustling hotel lobby, a melting pot of esports athletes from around the globe. The players milled about, clad in their colourful team jerseys amidst BattleScarz-themed decorations. The lively ambiance, reminiscent of pre-game virtual lobbies where they'd spent countless hours equipping their avatars, set the stage for the grand event ahead.

As Arjan queued at reception, friendly fire landed in the form of a beefy arm around his shoulders. "Welcome to Munich, Skip!" boomed a voice he'd recognize anywhere.

Arjan spun around, stepping back to take in the sight of his friend. A wide grin spread across his face. "Ah! Doc? Finally."

"It's so good to see you, Habibi!" Faiz exclaimed, stepping forward to draw Arjan into a bear hug that almost lifted him off the ground.

"You're way bigger than FaceTime led me to believe," Arjan managed to quip, his words nearly squished out of him by the strength of Faiz's embrace.

Setting Arjan back on solid ground, Faiz glanced down at himself. "Really? Does the camera add ten pounds or shed them?"

"You're looking great, man," Arjan assured with a genial smile.

"Thanks. You're not looking too bad yourself," Faiz shot back with a wink.

Before long, Eitan and Zafar spotted Arjan, their faces lighting up as they hurried over to pull him into a hug.

"Welcome to Germany!" Eitan greeted.

"Damn! It's so good to finally meet you guys," Arjan said, his excitement evident.

It was a surreal moment. The avatars they knew so intimately seemed to have leapt out of battle screens, transforming into real people. It was overwhelming, even a little awkward at first.

"How was your flight?" Zafar asked, eager to swap tales.

"Not bad. Yours? When did you guys get here?" Arjan asked.

"About an hour ago," Faiz said.

"Eitan got here first," Zafar pointed out with a grin.

"No surprises there," Arjan said, turning to Eitan. "The jetlag must be killing you."

"Long-haul flights are brutal, man. I'm so frazzled," Eitan replied in the same vein, feigning a yawn.

Arjan playfully punched his arm.

"Cut it out. That joke's so tired," Faiz said.

"By the way, you've got to see the practice bay they've set up here. It's pretty lit," Eitan said.

"Really? Can't wait!" Arjan replied, but his eyes scanned the room. "Where's Sahin?"

"Sahin hasn't arrived yet," Zafar said.

"What?" Arjan frowned, falling silent.

"We thought you'd know," Faiz said.

"Her flight was supposed to land this morning," Arjan said, a note of worry creeping in.

"Where is she, then? Why not call her?" Eitan suggested.

"Her phone's off," Arjan said, checking his phone again. "That's odd. Her flight landed on time."

"When did you last talk to her?" Zafar asked, his brows knitting together.

"Yesterday," Arjan replied, his breath quickening as he fidgeted nervously with a velvet ring box in his pocket.

Zafar and Eitan exchanged uneasy glances.

"She probably never got on that plane. I told you; her family wouldn't let her come," Eitan blurted, wasting no time to jump on the panic wagon. "Oh God, how are we supposed to win without her?"

"Are you serious right now?" Arjan snapped as his frown deepened.

"Calm down. She's not ditching us," Faiz said firmly, trying to diffuse the tension.

"Maybe she missed her flight or something," Zafar suggested, trying to sound hopeful.

"Exactly. It's not like the finale is tomorrow; she's got time. She'll be here," Faiz assured, his tone calming.

"Then why is her phone off?" Arjan asked, almost pleading for a comforting response.

"Stop overthinking. Phones run out of battery all the time, or maybe it's bad reception," Faiz said, aiming to soothe Arjan's frayed nerves.

"Her family probably seized her phone and grounded her," Eitan speculated, edging toward paranoia.

"Someone shut him up!" Arjan muttered in frustration.

"Why would she ghost us, then?" Eitan pressed.

"Just ignore him," Faiz said, stepping in front of Arjan. Resting his hands on Arjan's shoulders, he added firmly, "She's fine. She'll be here in no time. Trust me."

It took a moment for Arjan to nod, albeit hesitantly, as he tried to push aside his worries.

"Great! Let's head to the stadium," Faiz said, attempting to redirect their focus.

"I haven't even checked in yet," Arjan said, gesturing toward the reception.

"C'mon! We're late for the opening ceremony. We'll get you checked-in later," Faiz insisted, grabbing Arjan's luggage and dragging it to the bell desk.

Arjan hesitated, eyeing the unattended desk. "But it's unguarded."

"Relax! Nobody's stealing your precious bag," Faiz said.

"How many worries can you juggle at once?" Zafar teased.

With a resigned shrug, Arjan followed his friends out of the lobby.

* * *

As the Aces stepped into the Munich stadium, they were awestruck. The iconic venue, alive with dazzling lights and vibrant energy, felt like stepping into another world. At every turn, they were met with fascinating sights: the show floor resembled a miniature theme park, decked out with video game set-pieces and larger-than-life action figurines. It was a full house as hundreds of fans cosplayed in their favourite characters' costumes.

"Oh wow! Did we just walk into the game?" Eitan said, his eyes wide with wonder.

The line between virtual and real blurred as in-game items and mascots defected to the real world. Among them, Nuke Knight, the mascot of *BattleScarz*, stood in whimsical armour with a Nerf gun, surrounded by fans clamoring for selfies with the beloved character.

"Welcome to the opening night of the World Gaming Championship 2014!" the commentator's voice boomed across the stadium. Performers in dazzling costumes danced at the centre stage, moving to the beats spun by DJ Unicorn. Around them, twenty jumbotrons promised an immersive experience. The atmosphere hit a fever pitch as the iconic *BattleScarz* theme blasted through massive speakers, drawing deafening cheers from the crowd.

Amid the spectacle, Arjan was glued to his phone, anxiously checking Sahin's status and firing off messages.

Faiz, noticing, snatched the phone from his hands with a quick tug. "Stop obsessing! She's fine, trust me. You're missing the fun," Faiz said.

As Arjan lunged to grab his phone back, the ring box tumbled from his pocket. Faiz's eyes widened as Arjan hastily scooped it up and stuffed it back.

"Are you serious, dude?" Faiz blurted out, his jaw dropping.

Arjan shot him a pleading look, silently urging him to lower his voice.

Faiz whispered, "You're proposing already? You haven't even met her yet! Aren't you rushing into this?"

Arjan's face burned crimson, and he leaned in closer, his voice low. "I know it might seem a bit rushed, but I've never been surer about anything. She's the one…"

Before he could finish, Eitan appeared, weaving through the crowd with a six-pack of Bavarian beer.

"Here you go. A little liquid courage to take the edge off our anxieties," Eitan said, setting the beers down with a loud clink.

The sound pulled Zafar from the big screens as he turned to his friends and hollered, "Just what the doctor ordered!"

Casting a brief, almost scandalized look at the beers, Faiz muttered under his breath, "Not this doctor."

Arjan took a swig of the hefeweizen, hoping to drown the knot of worry in his chest.

Faiz redirected his piercing gaze to Arjan, still grappling with the speed of his romantic decisions. "Slow the hell down, my friend," he muttered.

"What? He just took one sip," Zafar said, confused.

"I'm not talking about the beer," Faiz replied dryly.

Zafar frowned while Arjan flashed a sheepish smile, silently pleading for the scrutiny to end.

Sensing his discomfort, Faiz shrugged. "Nothing," he said lightly, finally letting it slide.

Zafar, still puzzled but rolling with the flow, offered Faiz a pint.

Faiz politely declined, "I don't drink, my friend."

"Ah! I get it," Zafar nodded.

"What?" Faiz asked.

"That's haram. Those who drink alcohol will burn in hell," Zafar joked, trying to keep a straight face.

Faiz shook his head, laughing, "C'mon."

Eitan, already a beer down and catching the tail end of the conversation, raised another bottle high. "To burning in hell, Prost!" he exclaimed, knocking back the beer in one go.

Taking a cue from Eitan's unabashed spirit, Zafar declared, "Now that's how you do it in Germany. Let's go!" He chugged his beer with gusto, while Faiz and Arjan watched their antics with amused embarrassment.

A little later, the Aces gained access to the players' deck. They were greeted by two state-of-the-art gaming stations separated by an imposing glass panel. Each station boasted high-end screens and the latest PlayStation consoles, beckoning them into the action. Their designated area proudly displayed their team's name emblazoned across the headrests of throne-like gaming chairs.

Arjan approached his chair, running his fingers over the raised letters spelling Squad Aces on the black leather. A spark lit his eyes as he chewed his lower lip, emotions swirling. This was it – the esports stage he'd dreamt of. Settling into the chair, he surveyed the arena, imagining the intensity of game day. The thought sent a rush of adrenaline coursing through him.

Faiz tapped his shoulder gently. "A dream come true, isn't it? Can't believe we're here," he said, his voice filled with pride.

Arjan's eyes misted as he managed a shaky smile.

"It's been a long time coming," Zafar added.

"I'm so psyched! I can't wait for the finale," Eitan exclaimed.

As the Aces exchanged fist bumps, Faiz's gaze shifted to the adjacent station, where an all-Chinese squad had arrived. "Look who just showed up," he muttered, nodding toward the group.

Through the glass, they watched five young men in orange jerseys inspecting their station with an air of supremacy. Their skipper, Xiang, caught sight of the Aces and shot a cold, hostile glare.

"Shanghai Trojans, the defending champions," Eitan said, awe evident in his eyes.

"Everyone's pegging them to win again. In the qualifiers, they didn't let their opponents even catch a sniff," Zafar added with respect.

"How about you ask them for a selfie?" Faiz deadpanned.

"Or an autograph," Arjan said.

"What do you mean?" Eitan asked, confused.

"Stop fanboying. They're rivals. How do you expect to beat them when you're this starstruck," Faiz reasoned.

"They may be champions, but they're not invincible," Arjan said confidently.

"Exactly," Faiz agreed.

"I guess when a team keeps winning, the cracks go unnoticed. No team has counterattacked them. Wait till complacency sets in – then we pull the trigger," Arjan explained.

"Inshallah!" Faiz said with a firm nod.

"That's your master plan? Easier said than done," Eitan muttered.

Out of nowhere, Zafar remarked, "By the way, don't they all look alike?"

"Bruh, that's kind of racist," Eitan said, frowning.

Zafar's jaw dropped. "How dare you call me that?"

"Actually, they're related, brothers and cousins, like a Family Feud team," Faiz interjected.

"See? I was right. Don't ever call me that again," Zafar said, his voice carrying both vindication and a note of warning to Eitan.

"Sorry, my bad," Eitan muttered, taken aback by the trivia.

"Ah, the bickering couple strikes again. I won't be surprised if one of you ends up killing the other before this trip is over," Arjan sighed.

"If that happens, we'll be Quad-Aces again," Faiz quipped, his tone laced with dark humour as he referenced their original team name before Sahin's inclusion. The joke drew laughter from the group.

The party stretched far into the night as the Aces reveled in each other's company, swapping stories and jokes. By the time they returned to the hotel, Zafar and Eitan were visibly inebriated, their laughter echoing as they stumbled along. In contrast, Faiz, sober as a pilgrim, guided them to their rooms with steady steps. Arjan had indulged in a few drinks too many, yet not enough to quell his obsessive worry over Sahin, especially after Faiz had returned his phone. The messages were still unread, and her WhatsApp status hadn't changed all day.

7
Quad Aces

The morning rain drummed steadily against the hotel room window melding seamlessly with the deep slumber induced by the remnants of alcohol still coursing through Arjan's system. The peaceful melody was broken by a jarring ringtone. With eyes shut, he flailed toward the disturbing noise, his fingers scrabbling around the bedside table until they brushed against the cold, metallic surface of his iPhone. He blindly silenced it with the accuracy of a habitual snooze button tap. The respite was short-lived. Another bell went off, this one cutting through the remaining fog of sleep with its peculiar tone. The landline in his room, a relic seldom used, demanded action with an unsettling urgency. *It could be Sahin*. The thought jolted him awake. He immediately sat up and snatched up the receiver.

Before Arjan could speak, Faiz's tense voice crackled through. "Arjan! Turn on the TV. Channel 7," he said, his words tumbling out in a frantic cascade.

Arjan's confusion momentarily stalled his reply. "Slow down, Doc! What happened?"

"It's about Sahin," came the grim reply.

"What about her?" Arjan demanded, fear creeping in.

"Her hometown… it's been attacked by the Islamic State."

The news hit Arjan with the force of a tidal wave. "Oh my God! What are you talking about?" he stammered.

"Turn on the news. You'll see."

The line went dead, leaving a dense silence in its wake.

Heart pounding, Arjan fumbled for his glasses and rummaged through the sheets for the remote. His trembling fingers powered on the TV.

The screen flickered on, revealing a sombre-faced news anchor. "The Kurdish town of Kobani is under siege by the Islamic State," she reported, her voice steady but grave. "Civilians have been dragged from their homes and mercilessly beheaded. Countless women have been raped."

Arjan sat frozen, the remote clenched in his hand as the horror unfolded. Grabbing his phone, he tried calling Sahin, but her phone was still off. A sickening wave of terror welled up in him that forced him to his feet. He began pacing the confines of his room, the anchor's words echoing in his mind.

In a desperate search for answers, he called Faiz. "I can't reach her. Her phone's still off," Arjan said, his voice breaking.

"I tried too," Faiz replied, equally grim.

"It's bad, isn't it? She's… she's in danger," Arjan asked, a lump forming in his throat.

"I need my laptop and gear to track her devices. Without them, I can't do much," Faiz explained.

"What do we do? How will we find her?"

"Eitan knows someone in Munich who can help me with the tools. We're heading there now," Faiz said.

"I hope she's okay," Arjan murmured, choking back tears.

"Arjan! We don't know anything yet. Just pray and hope for the best," Faiz urged.

"I want to come along. I feel so helpless. I'll lose my mind just sitting here."

"We're already on the way. I promise we'll figure this out," Faiz said, then added firmly, "Hope always! Just like Sahin says."

Arjan echoed the words in a broken whisper, "Hope always." As he set down the phone, tears spilled over. He slumped into a chair, burying his head in his hands, overwhelmed by the torturous weight of uncertainty.

* * *

In the chaotic aftermath of Iraq's invasion, ISIS emerged from Al-Qaeda's shadow. It rapidly festered into a globally feared terror organization, having swept across vast swaths of the region with unprecedented brutality. It was so extreme that even Osama bin Laden distanced himself, seeking to salvage Al-Qaeda's reputation. Nothing spells 'evil' more resoundingly than being disowned by an outfit responsible for the most consequential terrorist attacks in the history of mankind.

At its helm was a firebrand cleric, enigmatic and zealous, who declared a self-styled caliphate sprawling across Iraq and Syria. This was no ordinary power grab; it was a mission to establish an Islamic theocracy and ignite a holy war as prophesied in ancient scriptures. The world watched in horror as this doctrine was demonstrated through the merciless spectacle of public executions.

Kobani, a Kurdish stronghold near the Syria-Turkey border, soon found itself in ISIS's crosshairs. Capturing Kobani was a strategic move for ISIS, offering control over key border crossings. It was but inevitable that the Kurds, the unintended defenders of this conflict, would find themselves in ISIS's path. The Kurdish people, regarded as one of the Middle East's original inhabitants, remain the largest stateless nation in the world. Their self-declared autonomous region, Rojava – born during the final throes of the Arab Spring, became a powerful emblem of defiance.

ISIS, fueled by wealth from captured oil fields and covert donations, wielded an arsenal of advanced weaponry, much of it seized from the routed Iraqi army. It had become a juggernaut of terror. In stark contrast, the Kurds, with limited resources, dwindling manpower, and outdated arms, seemed hopelessly outmatched. Yet their resistance emerged as a striking David-versus-Goliath narrative – except the disparity was even more staggering than the biblical tale. What began as a struggle for independence had transformed into a desperate battle for survival, capturing global attention and showcasing their resilience against a seemingly unstoppable terror machine.

*** * ***

Hunched over his chair, Arjan scattered messages across all of Sahin's social media profiles, clinging to the hope that one might break the unbearable quiet. It had been a torturous two days without a word from her, each hour stretching longer than the last. The news channel droned on, its updates on Kobani casting a grim backdrop to his mounting worry. He kept revisiting her last message, '*See you tomorrow, love. I can't believe we're finally meeting.*' What were once words of anticipation, now deepened the hollow ache in his heart. The absence of any response from Faiz, Eitan, and Zafar, who hadn't returned his calls, only heightened his sense of desolation.

The sudden knock on his door startled Arjan from his thoughts, sending a rush of hope through him. He sprang to his feet and swung the door open. Faiz, Zafar and Eitan stood solemnly before him.

"Did you find her?" Arjan asked, his voice thick with expectation.

The silence that met his question carried an ominous sense of foreboding. The trio entered slowly, their lowered heads conveying the unwelcome news he dreaded.

"What's wrong? Say something, did you find her?" Arjan pleaded, the suspense eating away at him.

They guided Arjan to the edge of the bed. Faiz sat across from him, while Eitan and Zafar stayed close, offering silent support.

"How bad is it? Just tell me," Arjan urged, bracing for the worst.

Faiz leaned forward, his voice low, "We managed to gain access to Sahin's console. There was a login today."

A flicker of hope crossed Arjan's face. "That's good news, right?" He searched their faces for reassurance.

"It wasn't her. It was someone else," Faiz revealed, sorrow heavy in his voice.

"How can you be so sure?" Arjan asked, a mix of denial and fear taking hold.

Faiz, clutching his throat, struggled with the words. "We tapped into their conversations. They were ISIS men... gloating about the looting, the violence, the horrors."

"And Sahin? Is she... is she..." Arjan's voice cracked as tears welled in his eyes.

Faiz met his gaze, his own eyes glistening, and slowly shook his head.

"Please, no..." Arjan begged, his plea dissolving into sobs as Eitan and Zafar placed firm, comforting hands on his shoulders.

"Her village was one of the first to fall. They did not get a chance to escape," Eitan lamented, his words carrying the weight of their collective sorrow.

Faiz reached out and embraced Arjan as he broke down, inconsolable. The others, too, were overwhelmed with emotion, sharing in the grief.

"Arjan, this is a big tragedy for all of us. We have to face it with courage," Zafar implored.

But Arjan's loss was too personal, his grief too profound for consolation.

8
Gamers Don't Die

That night, Germany triumphed over Argentina to clinch the 2014 FIFA World Cup, setting off wild celebrations across Munich. The long-awaited victory, ending a 24-year drought, was a historic moment for the nation. The city's veins pulsed with jubilant cheers, drumbeats, and clinking beer mugs, all swelling into a chorus of victory songs. Flags waved in a joyful frenzy and fireworks lit up the night sky, their booms softened by the walls of the hotel room that held Arjan captive in his grief.

Arjan slumped against the headboard, wrapped in a bubble of near silence, punctuated only by the muffled sounds of celebration seeping through. His eyes, red-rimmed and swollen, stared blankly into space, each wave of sorrow pulling him further from the world outside. Beside him, Faiz slept, his presence offering a faint solace, ensuring that he was not entirely alone in his darkest hour.

His gaze drifted to the nightstand where a small velvet box lay – a relic of a future that would never unfold. Trembling, he lifted the lid, the diamond ring inside weighing on his heart like a stone. Fresh tears clouded his vision as he ran a finger over the delicate engraving: '*Arjan ♡ Sahin.*' Each letter resonated like a harsh whisper of a dream that shattered too soon. Trapped in a foreign city that felt like a prison, Arjan wrestled with his thoughts amid the suffocating stillness. How could the world outside celebrate so freely while his own had come crashing down? As the clock struck midnight, his phone beeped – a reminder of the dinner reservation meant for two. The message, so innocuous yet so brutal, unraveled him further. As the night wore on, the glaring contrast between Munich's festive spirit and his profound despair deepened, making it an endless ordeal.

* * *

Next day, seeking closure and a sense of calm, Faiz, Eitan, and Zafar organized an in-game memorial stream for Sahin. News of her passing had spread like wildfire through the gaming circles, drawing players from across the globe to attend her virtual funeral in the very game world where they had come to know and cherish Sahin.

To maintain a respectful atmosphere, a specific code of conduct was established: all gamers were required to customize their avatars with plain black skins and mantles, a uniform of mourning. Thousands of these sombre avatars gathered at Halcyon Castle, now dimly lit by countless candles. The castle's flag, flown at half-mast, fluttered gently as if mourning the loss of its emperor.

The procession through the castle was a soul-stirring spectacle. Avatars moved in a remarkably orderly fashion along the narrow wall-walks. Upon reaching the Choppy Chapel, they queued at its entrance, which could accommodate only a hundred avatars at a time, patiently awaiting their turn to pay their respects. Since they did not know Sahin personally, they came to recognize and remember her through her avatar – a gender-neutral warrior, clad in a headscarf and face mask, with a bolt-action sniper slung across its back. In tribute, many expressed their grief creatively by spray-painting large murals of her avatar on the ancient stone walls. A commemorative headstone was erected atop the Topsie Tower, her favourite sniping spot, bearing the epitaph: '*Gamers don't die, they respawn.*' This quote, taken from Sahin's PlayStation bio, indulged the gamers' fantasy to emulate their avatars' magical ability to come back to life after death. If nothing else, it was a reverie that offered cold comfort to the grieving community.

Inside the chapel, avatars observed a moment of silence before laying virtual flowers and wreaths before a portrait of Sahin's avatar. The chapel, transformed into a place of digital reverence, echoed with the silent prayers of countless friends and fans. As they exited the game world, gamers poured their hearts out and paid homage. The chat box was deluged with tributes and heartfelt messages. Many entered the text code 'F', a virtual salute in the gaming community, to pay respect. The decorum displayed by such a large gathering marked a striking departure from the typically chaotic and toxic atmosphere of gaming lobbies. The voice chat remained respectfully quiet, save for a few important announcements like the resumption of the servers.

The colossal turnout for the stirring send-off overwhelmed the game servers, causing them to crash. The unprecedented traffic kept the developers on their toes as they worked tirelessly to keep them up and running. The gaming community had come together to create one of the grandest virtual funerals in the history of esports. Though, the setting of the funeral was virtual, the emotions were very real. It was unbelievable how many lives Sahin had touched during her brief and rather low-profile gaming career.

In his hotel room, Arjan watched the stream, surrounded by Zafar, Faiz, and Eitan. As tributes flooded social media, he blinked back tears, overwhelmed by the global outpouring of affection and respect for Sahin.

* * *

The grand finale had arrived, and the stage was set for the climactic showdown between the world's two finest teams, each vying for the most coveted esports trophy.

"Welcome to the finale of the World Championship," the commentator's voice rang out, reverberating through the packed stadium alive with anticipation.

Amid the sea of fans, a moving tribute stood out. The stands were decorated with elaborate tifos and gigantic posters featuring Sahin's avatar, while a striking fifty-foot mural dominated the backdrop, a vivid testament to the player's monumental impact on the game and its community.

The commentator's tone softened. "The tragic passing of Sahin has cast a shadow over today's celebration. The display of grief from his fans underscores the indelible legacy he has left behind. In honour of Sahin, we will now observe a moment of silence." As his words faded, the entire stadium fell silent—a powerful collective homage, with many spectators wearing black armbands in mourning.

As the minute passed, the commentator resumed, "But as they say, the show must go on. Today, Squad Aces face the Beijing Trojans. All eyes will be on the Aces when they make their entrance. With speculation swirling, everyone's asking: who will step up as the super-sub? Who will be deemed worthy enough to fill the big shoes of the legendary Sahin?"

The anticipation was electric, fans on the edge of their seats, eager for the drama to unfold in this emotionally charged clash of titans. A loud cheer erupted as the Beijing Trojans' anthem thundered through the speakers, their name blazing across the mega screens. Led by their captain, Xiang, the Chinese squad entered with a flourish of cold spark fountains framing their arrival.

"Beijing Trojans, the defending champions, have arrived!" the commentator declared.

As they made their way to the battle station, a tiny figure in the stands – a young girl of no more than five – reached out for Xiang's autograph. With a dismissive flick, he turned her away. His brash antics drew instant boos from the crowd, but Xiang seemed to be spurred on by the negative attention. As the Trojans settled into their station, the speakers crossfaded to the softened anthem of the Squad Aces.

The cheering shot up a notch as the announcer called them onto the stage, "Ladies and gentlemen, put your hands together for the Squad Aces."

As Zafar, Eitan, and Faiz entered the brightly lit indoor gaming stadium, they were accompanied by Emery, the substitute stepping in for their fallen teammate Sahin. A twenty-year-old wiry blonde from Munich and a close friend of Eitan, Emery had played a crucial role in helping the Aces track Sahin's console. The cameras closed in on his face as the enormity of the moment seemed to wash over him, an overwhelming blend of nerves and spotlight. Emery was not a professional gamer, so he had never faced the pressures of competitive play at this level. This was not just any game; it was the summit of the esports world, and his debut in such a high-stakes environment. What made it disconcerting was that even with Emery's inclusion, the Squad Aces were still one player short. Arjan was conspicuous by his absence. All eyes kept darting toward the entrance, puzzled by his no-show.

"We regret to inform you that the captain of Squad Aces has apparently withdrawn from the tournament, citing personal reasons, and has left for his home country," the commentator announced, his tone heavy with disappointment. "Further details will be shared as they become available."

The news rippled through the crowd, turning cheers into a collective sigh of dismay. It was a major blow to the Aces and a buzzkill for the spectators who had come to watch a riveting contest. Even at full strength, the Aces were viewed as underdogs against the formidable Trojans, with betting odds stacked heavily against them. Now, with Arjan missing, the matchup seemed destined to become a bloodbath. Aware of the significant advantage this development had afforded them, the Trojan players exchanged smug smirks, licking their lips at the prospect of a walkover.

"It's a disgrace that this marquee event has turned into a one-sided affair from the outset," the commentator lamented, setting a grim tone for what was to be the year's most anticipated esports match.

As the lights dimmed and the game kicked off, the Aces' sombre expressions conveyed the gravity of their predicament. The vacant chair beside them was a constant sting, a stark reminder of their incomplete lineup. Wasting no time, the Trojans leveraged their numerical advantage with aggressive, coordinated attacks, overwhelming the Aces. Despite the team's spirited efforts, the absence of Sahin and Arjan left a void too great to fill. The first game ended decisively in the Trojans' favour.

"Trojans have blown the Aces out of the water," the commentator announced as the first round concluded far earlier than expected.

The Aces hung their heads, weighed down by the dismal start. With ten minutes before the next round, Faiz stood up and stormed off to the locker room.

The commentator's tone softened, reflecting a mix of empathy and respect. "Fans must salute the great courage of the Aces. They could have forfeited, yet they chose to turn up and fight, even with just four players."

Meanwhile, ten kilometres from the arena, Arjan sat in the back of a taxi hurtling along the German autobahn. The signage for *'München International Airport'* loomed ahead as he gazed vacantly out the window, the blur of the landscape barely registering in his troubled mind. The shrill ringtone of an incoming call interrupted his thoughts. 'Faiz calling' flashed on the screen. Arjan stared at the display for a long moment, his emotions torn. Finally, with a heavy heart, he tapped the decline button. Setting the phone down, he clasped his hand to his forehead, writhing with guilt for having abandoned his team at such a critical juncture. Moments later, his phone buzzed again, this time with a new message. Arjan hesitated, reluctant to confront the reality he had tried to leave behind, before unlocking the screen.

It was a text from Faiz, *'It's tough here without you, skipper. The team's morale is low. Would it be possible for you to join us for a quick FaceTime?*

Just hearing your voice might lift the boys up. It would give us strength to at least put up a fight. Thanks, man.'

Arjan's eyes welled up as he clutched the phone, a wave of emotions threatening to overcome him. He typed back with labored keystrokes, *'I'm really sorry, Faiz. I'm not in a place to talk right now. Please tell the team I'm with them in spirit. Best of luck, and apologies.'*

Faiz responded, *'It's okay, man. I understand. Take care.'*

His words were tinged with disappointment, not at Arjan but at the cruel twist of fate. With a heavy heart, Faiz pocketed his phone and slowly made his way back to the battle station, feeling the burden of leadership weigh down on him more than ever in Arjan's absence.

The second round commenced, and the script was dishearteningly familiar. Only minutes in, the Trojans were decimating them from every angle. The Squad Aces' supporters watched in stunned silence as the carnage played out on the jumbotrons. Short-handed and demoralized, the Aces seemed to crumble under the relentless pressure; their faces etched with the inevitability of defeat.

What made the drubbing even more unbearable to watch was how the Trojans were unnecessarily flogging the dead game. Toying with their opponents, they let incapacitated players slowly bleed out in a drawn-out agony instead of delivering quick kills. Worse still, they taunted them with each blow, adding insult to injury. It's almost frightening how humans can behave when there is no risk of retribution.

"We expect better from the defending champions. A bit more grace, especially toward the bereaved," the commentator said, his tone heavy with displeasure.

Unable to stomach the unsightly treatment, many spectators began leaving the stadium in dismay. Though the Trojans were on track for a second consecutive title, having won two of the five rounds, their despicable conduct cost them the respect of fans.

Just as the atmosphere had soured to its lowest, a sudden stir at the entrance drew everyone's attention. Arjan stepped in, like a messiah in their moment of need. His unexpected arrival ignited a surge of hope among the disheartened supporters, sparking thunderous cheers that rippled across the stands. His beleaguered teammates sprang to life, their faces lighting up with relief and gratitude, as if his presence had breathed new energy into their battered spirits.

The commentator scrambled to keep up. "And what do we have here? Just when all seemed lost for the Aces, their captain returns! Could this be the turning point, or is it too little, too late?"

Arjan strode past the bewildered Trojans, his focused gaze locking with his teammates. The match, once seemingly decided, now bristled with new possibilities. The psychological warfare the Trojans had waged, threatened to backfire spectacularly.

As he reached the Aces' deck, Eitan handed him the team jersey, his hands trembling with emotion. Arjan slipped it on, the sight steeling the team's resolve. The Aces rallied around him, their unity fierce, like a wounded tiger ready to turn on its hunter.

"Thank you, skipper," Faiz said, his voice thick with emotion.

"One squad, one mind," Arjan said, his voice catching in his throat.

"No Ace left behind," the squad completed, their motto weighted with bitter irony.

"Let's do this – one last time. For Sahin," Arjan declared, his voice a resonant call to arms that rekindled a fire in his team's eyes.

The cameras zoomed in on Arjan's determined expression, sparking a surge in global viewership as fans tuned in to witness the potential comeback. With seconds left before the next round, he donned his headset and claimed the once-vacant chair. There was no time for reunions; it was about channelizing all their energy on turning the tide. Even if it was too late to win, they were driven to reclaim their honour.

The crowd erupted in support of the Aces. Even some Trojans' fans, disillusioned by their own team's tactics, found themselves drawn to the underdogs in a stunning shift of allegiances.

Arjan's impact was immediate. He restructured their formation and unleashed a fierce offense that left the Trojans reeling. The Chinese defence was not prepared to handle such a resolute rear-guard action. The Aces celebrated each point with impassioned intensity, clawing their way toward an unlikely reversal. Seeing the game slip away, Xiang's temper flared dramatically. He hurled his controller and lashed out at his defenders. His outburst sent ripples of discord through their ranks – cracks the Aces were all too eager to exploit.

Arjan was a man possessed. Playing the game of his life, his stoic gaze remained fixed on the screen, his expression impassive, almost robotic. As he navigated the map, his movements were fluid and lethal. Each headshot delivered with Sahin's favoured sniper rifle felt like a tribute to his fallen partner. His fingers danced across the gaming controller, as if his being subliminally knew this was his last dance. Perhaps, his best was always meant for now.

Led by his exploits and masterful orchestration, the Aces took control of the game. Though the score was now even, the Trojans were already beaten in spirit. Dazed and disoriented, they looked like deer caught in headlights, unable to process the force that had hit them.

By the final round, the outcome was clear – a complete rout. The Trojans, their composure shattered and leadership in disarray, scrambled to defend.

In the final moments of the game, as Arjan lined up the championship-winning shot, the entire stadium held its breath. Then, as he executed the kill, a thunderous wave of applause burst forth, cascading through the arena.

"Ladies and gentlemen, take a bow! Squad Aces are the world champions! This has been an unbelievable turn of events… a huge applause for the team!" the commentator's voice boomed.

Overwhelmed by the moment, the Aces thumped their chests, each strike a visceral expression of triumph and bittersweet catharsis. Their dream had come true, but under circumstances that made the victory feel both heavy and profound.

At the post-match ceremony, Arjan's voice trembled. "This victory belongs to Sahin. We dedicate this trophy to the one without whom we wouldn't be standing here today," he declared, his words a heartfelt tribute met with a standing ovation.

The team ascended the podium and lifted the gleaming silverware high amid a blizzard of confetti raining down on them. As a montage of Sahin's gameplay lit up the jumbotrons, the Aces were overcome with emotion. Tears streamed down their faces as they gathered for one final huddle. They wrapped their arms tightly around each other, grappling with the intense emotions of impending separation. This was more than just a team; it was a family forged through shared trials and triumphs. Each sob echoed the deep bond they had formed – a bond that would soon be a memory as they prepared to go their separate ways. It marked the end of an era for the Squad Aces, a heartrending farewell to a chapter as beautiful as it was fleeting. They had not only secured the championship but also immortalized the legacy of a beloved player, forever cementing their place in the annals of esports history.

9
…They Respawn

A month had passed since the surreal championship night when Arjan hoisted the trophy amid blinding camera flashes, media frenzy, and deafening fanfare. Now, half a world away, the contrast couldn't be starker. Cooped up in his room, Arjan slouched in an oversized t-shirt and grimy pajamas, neglect etched into every detail. His beard was overgrown, his hair unkempt, and dark circles under his eyes aged him beyond his years. Grief had shattered him, leaving pieces he hadn't begun to gather. At his feet, Mario lay listlessly, mirroring his owner's sorrow. In the background, the hum of a news channel droned on, as unnoticed as the dust settling on his abandoned gaming rig.

Arjan sat despondently on the couch, staring blankly out the window as the news anchor's voice melded into the white noise. "The jihadists of Islamic State believe in a fable that if they die as martyrs, they will be rewarded with seventy-two eternal virgins in heaven. But if killed by a woman, they will be sent straight to hell."

On TV, a citizen journalist reported from the front lines: "This belief is why more and more women are joining the fight against ISIS, turning the doctrine against them."

The journalist moved through the encampment with her camera crew, approaching a group of young Kurdish women fighters. Armed yet exuding quiet strength, the fighters greeted her with warm smiles, ready to share their stories.

"These brave women are the focus of our feature today," the journalist said, introducing them. Turning to one of the fighters, she asked, "Can you explain how you're using the enemy's own beliefs against them?"

The fighter nodded, her expression resolute. "Whenever we shoot down a Daesh fighter, we let out high-pitched celebratory sounds so ISIS knows their comrade was killed by a woman, denying them martyrdom. It shatters their morale. They don't want to die by our bullets – it gives us a psychological edge."

The journalist nodded with quiet admiration before turning the microphone to another fighter. "We are an egalitarian group, and this fight allows us to challenge patriarchal norms while striving for equality in our society. After all, we ensure Daesh fighters meet their end without the glory they expect."

"Now, let's meet one of the most celebrated Kurdish fighters," the journalist continued. "She goes by the nom de guerre 'Hell Cat'. True to her name, she has sent at least thirty Daesh fighters to hell. Let's hear from the sniper who never wastes a bullet," she announced as the camera focused on a determined figure within the group.

"We're running out of weapons and ammunition. That's why I prefer headshots," the fighter's words cut through Arjan's haze of thoughts, startling him with their uncanny familiarity. He sat up and stared into the screen. That voice… it couldn't be…

Arjan froze, his eyes widening in disbelief. On the screen was none other than Sahin – alive!

Clad in military fatigues with a scarf loosely draped around her neck, she looked battle-hardened yet unmistakably herself. The sight of her sent a jolt through Arjan, like an adrenaline shot to his system. He stood up, his pulse quickening. Even Mario, sensing the shift in energy, perked his ears and tilted his head, watching his owner with curious concern.

"One shot, one kill. A headshot saves bullets, and every bullet is as precious as gold," Sahin continued, her voice steady with characteristic bravado.

Arjan's breath hitched as tears of joy streamed down his face. The grief that had consumed him for weeks dissolved into an overwhelming flood of relief. Sahin – the love he thought he'd lost forever – was alive. Spellbound, he couldn't look away, unable to fully grasp the staggering reality unfolding before him.

But the joy was fleeting. Sahin wasn't just alive – she was locked in a deadly battle against the world's most dangerous terror group. Arjan's thoughts spiraled, the weight of her peril crushing the brief relief of her survival. Restless, he paced the room, his mind racing. What could he do to help Sahin escape this dire situation? The thought of her in harm's way was unbearable. Time was slipping away – every second critical. The Kurdish forces were under relentless attack, their resources stretched thin.

Arjan couldn't sit idle. Sahin needed him. No matter the odds… no matter the cost, he had to find a way to reach her. To protect her. He did not have a plan, but he knew one thing – he could not and would not stand by while she faced this nightmare alone.

* * *

As the hours ticked by, Arjan remained engrossed in his research, the room around him dimming as night fell. Mario slept soundly amidst the quiet chaos of what had become Arjan's makeshift command centre. The dusty Nerf gun and a pile of journalism books had been shoved aside to make space for a sprawl of maps across his desk. Multiple tabs on his computer screen glowed with the latest updates from the conflict zone. His eyes, rarely blinking, absorbed the deluge of information as he sipped endless cups of coffee, trying to channel his mounting anxiety into a coherent rescue plan.

He compiled a list of NGOs operating in Kurdistan, sending heartfelt pleas for help with evacuation efforts in Kobani. Yet, hope remained elusive. Depending on outsiders with no personal stake in the crisis left him feeling increasingly detached. The more he consumed articles and footage about ISIS, the more his optimism eroded. To the rest of the world, it seemed, Kobani's plight was merely a piece of news, ignored and quickly forgotten.

Faiz's message buzzed on his phone: *'Analyzing metadata from the interview clip – it's local. No timestamps yet, need more time to pinpoint the exact location. Chatter on the dark web hints at an imminent ISIS push. If she's still there, time's running out.'*

Arjan stared at the screen, a heavy knot forming in his stomach as unease gripped him. There was no time to rely on outside help. Without any skin in the game, his plan risked becoming nothing more than a wishful fantasy. Determined, he turned to his computer and typed *'How to travel to Syria?'* into the search bar. He carefully pored over the results. Sensing the inherent dangers in his original query, he refined it by editing it to *'How to travel safely to Syria?'* and placing quotation marks around *"safely"* to weed out riskier options. The search results were sparse, as if even Google balked at the idea of safe passage into a war zone. Drained, he slumped back in his chair, watching the first rays of dawn creep through the window, shedding a sobering light on the harsh truth: he had only begun to scratch the surface of a daunting mission.

The unusual early morning activity in Arjan's room caught his mother's attention as she passed by. A flicker of concern crossed her face, prompting her to knock gently.

"Arjan, are you awake?" Anita called softly.

"Yes, Mumma," he replied, surprised by the knock.

"So early? What are you doing?" she probed, easing the door open.

"Just studying," he said, straightening in his chair, trying to mask his weariness.

Anita stepped inside, her wet hair neatly tucked in a towel, wearing an elegant ethnic maroon suit. Her tidy appearance sharply contrasted with both Arjan and his disorderly room. Her gaze swept over the desk littered with articles on guerrilla warfare, annotated maps, and hastily scribbled notes. Although the chaos made her heart flip, she was heartened to see Arjan so focused, something she hadn't quite seen since he returned from Munich. For her, finding him awake early and buried in books was the stuff of dreams.

"Studying for an exam?" she inquired lightly, trying to make sense of the mess.

"Yes, Mumma," Arjan replied, keeping his answers simple to ease her concerns.

"From the looks of it, seems like the toughest exam of your life," she joked.

Arjan pondered the unintended irony in the remark she had casually dropped. After a moment, he smiled and said, "Moms know everything, don't they?"

A playful twinkle lit up in Anita's eyes. "Well, your father hasn't even woken up yet. I can't wait to tease him that you were up before him."

Arjan managed a weary grin.

"Should I send some breakfast and tea?" she offered.

"Not now, I'll have it in a while, Mumma," he replied

"By the way, your room is quite a disaster, but have you looked at yourself? When did you last take a bath?" she asked, her tone lightly scolding.

"Mumma, please, not now. Let me study," he pleaded.

"Okay, okay," she relented. As she turned to leave, she picked up the empty coffee mugs from his desk and asked casually, "By the way, what's your exam on?"

"War reporting," he replied, blurting out the first topic that came to mind.

"War reporting?" she repeated, her gaze flicking to the annotated map of Syria. With a playful raise of her eyebrows, she teased, "On the first assignment, are they sending your batch directly to Syria or what?" A chuckle escaped her, clearly amused by her own jest.

Annoyed by his mother's sprightly banter so early in the morning, he grumbled, "Mom, why crack dad jokes, that too first thing in the…" His voice trailed off, his eyes widening with sudden realization.

Oblivious, Anita smiled. "Okay, Baba, I'll leave you to it. I'll have Raju bring a strawberry smoothie for you." She walked out, unaware of the spark her light-hearted comment had ignited in Arjan's mind.

Her words hung in the air as Arjan sat back, the gears turning in his head. *Cover the war in Syria? That was it.* A way to get on the ground, close to where Sahin might be. Journalism could be his cover, a legit guise to enter the war zone. His mother's offhand joke had unlocked a viable pathway. Global media often relied on local survivors or citizen journalists to report from the most dangerous conflict zones, including Syria and Iraq. This was notoriously the most dangerous place in the world for journalists. In fact, many had lost their lives to ISIS. Arjan thought to himself that this was his best chance – of course, not to seek danger, but to leverage his journalistic credentials to gain access to Kobani. If he could secure backing from a reputable media house, he might get the visa and clearance he needed. It was a long shot, but that was all he had. The risks were high, but for Sahin, Arjan was ready to face whatever lay ahead.

* * *

After days of neglect, Arjan had transformed. A hot shower and trim worked wonders, pulling him back from the brink of the Stone Age. Now, dressed sharply in formal attire, he sat in the reception area of the news channel INDIA365, its vibrant signage flickering above a garish desk.

Arjan sat with quiet determination, exuding a calm confidence unusual for someone at their first-ever job interview. He knew the media thrived on sensationalism, and his pitch was crafted to perfection: a lone wolf journalist covering the Syrian war – a bold, dangerous assignment that any news outlet would seize to brand their next 'daredevil reporter'.

As the previous candidate exited the interview room, Arjan reached into his pocket, retrieved a nasal spray, and took a quick puff in each nostril. The receptionist, a pale woman, gestured for him to enter.

Straightening his jacket, Arjan rose and walked to the door with steady confidence. He stepped inside, greeting the interviewers with a polite smile. Pranab, a portly media mogul in his sixties with a flowing white beard, sat at one end of the table. Opposite him, Varsha, a celebrated war correspondent draped in an elegant saree, gave him a measured glance as he handed over his resume folder. They flipped through the folder, their expressions shifting subtly to suggest approval.

"Impressive. I see you've graduated from a prestigious journalism school," Varsha remarked, glancing at her co-interviewer with a knowing smile. "It just so happens to be his alma mater. Looks like you've already got a bit of a head start."

Pranab chuckled.

"That's great to know," Arjan replied, his smile broadening slightly.

"You've mentioned political reporting is your preferred beat," Varsha said.

"Yes, Ma'am," Arjan affirmed.

"It is a breath of fresh air to see someone take an active interest in politics," Pranab finally spoke, his voice deep and slightly hoarse.

"Indeed," Varsha agreed. "Most applicants today were interested in sports or technology reporting."

"One even mentioned… umm I'm forgetting. What was it?" Pranab paused, scratching his balding scalp.

"Video game journalism," Varsha scoffed.

Arjan scrunched his nose, offering a wry smile, feigning cluelessness.

"What does that even mean? What's wrong with this generation?" Pranab mused. Then, with a hint of pride, he added, "Just like test cricket is the real cricket, political journalism is the real journalism. Do you agree, young man?"

Arjan nodded politely.

"We're currently looking to fill a political correspondent role in

Bihar," Varsha revealed. "You'll be notified about the selection results in a few days."

"Thank you, but I'm not here for that position," Arjan said.

The interviewers exchanged puzzled glances.

"What do you mean?" Pranab asked.

"I came here with a proposition," Arjan began, leaning forward, his tone resolute.

Their curiosity piqued; they sat up slightly.

"I've been closely following the rise of ISIS in Syria and Iraq and the mayhem it's unleashed," Arjan explained passionately. "Hardly any Indian journalist has dared to report from ground zero. My proposal is this: I'm willing to go to Syria and report single-handedly on behalf of your channel."

The room fell silent as the interviewers absorbed his words.

Pranab's face contorted in exasperation. "This has to be the most preposterous proposition I've ever heard! Are you in your right mind?" he muttered.

"I'm a little curious," Varsha said, restraining herself as she tried to reason, "If you're such a braveheart to go alone, why have you come to us?"

"Having the support of a credible media house like yours would make securing a visa and managing logistics through Turkey significantly easier," Arjan responded.

Pranab interjected, visibly agitated, "Do you even hear yourself? Frankly, Mr Arjan, this is reckless and immature. No media house is going to hire a rookie and send him straight to Syria. How did you even think that this was going to work?"

"Sir, think about it. Your channel could be the first Indian channel to provide live, on-the-ground coverage of the Syrian war," Arjan persisted, his voice steady despite the rising tension.

"Mr Arjan, let me tell you something," Pranab said sternly. "The reasons are aplenty why no Indian channel has covered the Syrian crisis directly, and none of them suggest that Indian journalists lack bravery."

"Sir. I never meant to imply…"

"Enough!" Varsha interrupted. "You're only making this harder for yourself."

Arjan faltered, his initial resolve fading under their critical gaze. "Ma'am, if you'd just hear me out…"

"I think we've heard enough, Mr Arjan," Pranab said, standing to signal the end of the interview. "Thank you for coming. You may leave now. *Kahan se aa jaate hain…*" he added, shaking his head.

Humiliated and dejected, Arjan left the room, his footsteps slow, his spirit crushed by the blunt rejection. This was not the first time Arjan had been turned away so unceremoniously after presenting his dangerous proposition. Over the next few days, he approached multiple news outlets, only to face a string of similar rejections. Each refusal echoed louder than the last, compelling him to face the painful truth: his plan was rash and half-cocked, and unlikely to gain support. It became clear that he needed a new strategy. A strategy that was deliberate and better thought out, if he was to have any chance of rescuing Sahin.

★ ★ ★

Arjan sat distraught at his cluttered study desk, surrounded by paperwork and his passport, meticulously filling out the Republic of Turkey visa form. With no media house showing interest in his original pitch, he had resolved to move forward with an altered plan. Despite countless unanswered emails to NGOs and government entities, his exhaustive research into Kurdistan's humanitarian efforts had not been in vain after all. Among the promising leads was Medics Without Borders, an organization actively seeking volunteer nurses to provide aid in Syrian towns. In just six days, the group was set to gather in the Turkish city of Suruç to negotiate permits for crossing into Syria. To blend in, Arjan forged a certificate as a registered nurse, presenting himself as a qualified paramedic. He carefully organized his travel documents, ensuring every detail was flawless for submission at the consulate.

His focus was abruptly shattered by the television blaring breaking news:

'Turkey closes border crossing with Syria.'

With bated breath, Arjan raised the volume as the newsreader outlined the grim implications of the border closure. "The Kurds in Turkey are embittered as the tragedy of Kobani unfolds before their eyes on the other side of a wire fence and they can do nothing about it. In Syria, the Kurdish fighters of the YPG militia are beleaguered. They were unaided, apart from pinpricks of occasional western airstrikes. The US-led allies have been bombing Islamic State positions during the day, but it may not be enough to stifle ISIS."

The Turkey-Syria border was sealed, cutting off what he had thought was a viable route into the conflict zone. The closure was more than just a logistical setback – it was a reminder of the tangled geopolitical web he was up against. Turkey's proximity to Kobani made it a key player in the conflict, but its inaction was viewed by many as tacit support for ISIS and a betrayal of the Kurds. The reality, however, was far more complicated. Turkey saw both ISIS and the Kurds as threats, trapped in a catch-22 that prevented any direct intervention. This precarious balancing act left Kobani isolated and Turkey's motives under scrutiny, further complicating Arjan's fragile plans.

Every option Arjan considered seemed to crumble before him. Every turn led to a dead end, trapping him in an endless maze. Sitting alone with his head buried in his hands, he felt the crushing weight of inadequacy bear down on him.

I think it's time you gave up. You made plans. They failed. It's not your fault the media won't hire you. It's not your fault Turkey sealed the borders. It was never doable. Maybe this is a sign – God's way of telling you to stop.

Arjan's chest tightened as the voice pressed on, cruelly steady.

That's the signal, Arjan. You're no hero. No saviour. Just another fool clinging to a delusion, thinking you could fix this. She's strong – she doesn't need your saving. If she has to die, so be it. It's not on you. You won't have blood on your hands. Put it on God, I say. Blame Him. You're just the victim here, right? You tried, didn't you?

The voice grew harsher, dripping with venom.

Victim. That's reasonable, isn't it? Sit here, wallow in self-pity, and call it fate. Let her fight alone while you drown in your failures. She's risking her life, and all you've done is make plans that collapse at the first hurdle. Tell yourself it's fine. You tried. But would that make it easier when the regret starts eating you alive?

A surge of emotion broke through. His breath quickened, fists tightened, his body bracing against the storm within. *Don't worry, Arjan. I won't let you suffer even a shred of guilt. We'll tell ourselves we tried. We gave it all. But what else could we have done?*

Something inside him snapped. Arjan shot upright, sweeping the mess off his desk with a single motion. Maps, papers, and empty coffee cups clattered to the floor, the crash startling even himself. He stood there, trembling, the silence that followed ringing loud in his ears.

And then, the doorbell. A relentless barrage of rings jolted him out of his thoughts. Annoyed, he dragged himself toward the door, muttering under his breath, *why is no one answering the goddamn bell?*

The house was eerily quiet, and the persistent ringing quickened his steps. Reaching the door, he peered through the viewer. A figure stood on the other side – broad-shouldered, impeccably dressed in a tailored suit, his posture radiating authority. Arjan hesitated, then opened the door a crack.

The man offered no greeting, simply pulling out a small leather wallet and flipping it open to reveal an official badge.

"Ashar Khan, Intelligence Bureau," he said. The words fell like a weight in the air.

Arjan's heart raced. *The Intelligence Bureau? What do they want with me?*

10
Leap of Faith

Ashar Khan sat in his sparsely furnished office, sipping tea as a cricket match murmured on a small television in the corner. Beside him, his assistant, Joginder, a tubby man with an unassuming demeanor, assembled a dossier. Through the two-way mirror, they could see Arjan sitting alone in the stark interrogation room, hours of isolation visibly wearing on him.

"Sir! He seems innocent. Comes from a respectable family. *Jaane dijiye*," Joginder suggested gently.

Khan raised an eyebrow, his tone biting, "Oh, really?"

Joginder nodded earnestly.

Leaning back in his chair, Khan's voice turned cold and deliberate. "You know who else came from a respectable family?"

Joginder blinked, confused. "Who, Sir?"

"Osama Bin Laden," Khan said curtly, his tone heavy with finality.

After a brief pause, Joginder hesitated. "Sir, there's something else…"

"What now?" Khan asked impatiently.

Joginder drew a deep breath but thought better of it. "Nothing, Sir."

Khan, catching the hesitation, pressed, "I know what you're thinking. But ISIS doesn't recruit based on religion."

Joginder shifted uneasily. "Still, Sir, my gut feeling says he's innocent."

"Keep your gut to yourself and leave the interrogation to me," Khan snapped. Rising, he strode toward the interrogation room, Joginder trailing behind.

Khan sat across from Arjan in the dimly lit room, where a single bare ceiling lamp dangled ominously over Arjan's head. Joginder lingered quietly in a corner.

"Mr Arjan," Khan began, his tone dry, "we've learned about your plans to travel to Syria. Funny, I don't recall Syria being on anyone's best-places-to-visit-before-you-die list."

Joginder, unable to resist, chimed in, "It's probably on the best-places-to-visit-to-die."

Khan's glare snapped to Joginder, silencing him instantly. The smirk disappeared from Joginder's face, and he slunk further into the corner.

Khan turned his attention back to Arjan, his expression hardening. "So," he said coldly, "why Syria?"

Arjan fidgeted, avoiding eye contact. "I… I've been watching videos about ISIS. I wanted to…"

"That was quick," Khan cut in coldly. "You're confessing already?"

"No! I never said that," Arjan protested.

Khan leaned in, his voice dropping to a menacing growl. "Let me guess, you're number sixteen? Fifteen others have already left for Syria. Got left behind, did you?"

Arjan shook his head vehemently. "No, I swear! I have nothing to do with them!"

"Then why?" Khan demanded, his patience wearing thin.

Arjan exhaled shakily, then blurted out, "My girlfriend. She's missing there. I need to find her and save her from ISIS."

Silence hung thick in the room. Joginder exchanged a bewildered glance with Khan, who raised an eyebrow, then broke into a mocking laugh.

"Your girlfriend? In Syria? That's your story?" Khan scoffed, his voice dripping with derision.

Joginder let out a nervous chuckle but froze as Khan lunged forward and pounded the metal desk. "*Main tujhe chutiya dikhta hoon kya*?" (Do I look like a dumbfuck?)

Arjan recoiled, his voice trembling. "Sir! I'm telling the truth… please believe me."

"No rush," Khan said coldly, regaining composure. "We can sit here all night if you're not ready to come clean."

A sharp knock on the glass door interrupted him. The director, a stern, bald man, motioned for Khan to step out.

Khan gave a resigned nod, muttering under his breath, "Speak of the chu…" He trailed off, catching himself. Turning back to Arjan, he said, "I'll be back. Take your time." His sharp gaze lingered briefly before he exited the room with Joginder, the door clicking shut behind them.

In the adjacent cabin, the director stood with his arms crossed, his expression grave. "The kid's clean. We've scoured his devices thoroughly," he stated firmly.

Joginder, standing quietly behind Khan, secretly allowed himself a flicker of vindication.

Khan was unmoved. "Sir, have you seen his browsing history? ISIS propaganda videos, execution footage, daily searches for flights to Syria – it's all there. You can't ignore that."

"That's concerning, I agree, but it's not enough to detain him," the director countered.

"Sir, the backlash we've already faced for letting a bunch of them slip through… everyone's baying for our blood. His intent to travel to Syria is enough for me to make an example out of him," Khan argued. "He's contacting media outlets to facilitate his trip. For God's sake, there has to be something!"

"I get it. I'm not saying let him off the hook. Hold his passport and keep an eye on him. There is no evidence of anything else, so cut the kid some slack."

Khan nodded reluctantly. "As you say, Sir!"

"Then get back to it," the director commanded.

Shaking his head, Khan strode back into the interrogation room. Arjan straightened in his chair, visibly tense as Khan sat down, his expression unreadable.

"I believe you must be tired by now," Khan began, his tone unexpectedly soft.

Arjan blinked, surprised by the sudden mellowing.

"It's late," Khan continued, glancing at his watch. "We're not going to resolve anything tonight. One of our officers will drive you home."

"Thank you, Sir," Arjan replied, his relief cautious but palpable.

Khan's eyes narrowed slightly. "I'm not done yet. You'll need to come back tomorrow for further questioning. And I'll need your passport."

Arjan froze. Handing over his passport would sabotage any chance of saving Sahin. He needed a way out fast.

"Where are you lost?" Khan demanded, noticing Arjan's distraction.

Arjan snapped out of his thoughts. "I don't have my passport."

"Of course," Khan said dryly. "That's why one of our men will escort you to your house, drop you off and come back with your passport. Convenient, right?"

"I mean… I don't actually have it," Arjan stammered, playing for time.

"What do you mean you don't have it?"

Arjan's mind raced, his heart pounding. *Lost it? No. Misplaced it? They'll turn my house upside down. Think Arjan, THINK!*

"Don't test my patience," Khan said, irritation flaring.

"I… I'm sorry, Sir," Arjan stuttered, grasping at an excuse. "I think I'm just… exhausted."

"For the last time, where the hell is your passport?"

Arjan scratched his head, feigning confusion before a plausible excuse emerged. "It's at the consulate. I submitted it for a Turkey visa," he said, testing the waters. Seeing that his improv might just hold up, he pressed on with more conviction, "Yes, it's at the Turkish consulate."

Khan's expression darkened. "So, you were planning to get to Syria through Turkey?"

"No!" Arjan protested, his voice higher than he intended. "Nothing like that. I've been planning a trip to Istanbul for a while now. That's the only reason."

Khan raised an eyebrow. "A girlfriend there, too?"

"No, just sightseeing. Beautiful country," Arjan insisted, trying to sound casual.

Khan shook his head, not buying it. "We'll seize your passport from the consulate first thing tomorrow."

"When will I get it back?" Arjan asked, trying not to let his panic show.

Khan's tone turned blunt. "When we're convinced you're not booking any more suicidal trips. You're lucky we're not holding you in custody."

Arjan nodded solemnly.

"You may leave now," Khan dismissed.

"Okay. I'll get going then," Arjan said, rising to leave.

Khan handed him his iPhone. "We'll see you tomorrow."

Arjan nodded and walked out, his thoughts a chaotic swirl of relief and apprehension.

As he descended the stairs, his phone, now powered back on, buzzed incessantly with a flood of missed notifications. One caught his eye – an ominous news link from Zafar. His stomach churned as he tapped it.

The headline hit him like a punch: *'Kurdish women warriors captured in Kobani, face imminent execution.'*

Arjan's breath quickened. Nausea surged as the words sank in. Clutching the stair rail, he steadied himself, sweat trickling down his temple. He lurched into the nearest restroom, barely making it before retching violently.

He slumped against the sink so heavily it threatened to clatter loose. His trembling hands fumbled with the tap until cold water gushed out. He splashed it on his face, the frigid sting jolted his senses but did nothing to calm the storm raging in his mind.

★ ★ ★

Arjan knew his window of opportunity was closing fast. Heart pounding, he stormed out of the intelligence bureau and flagged down a taxi, diving into the first one that stopped. As the cab sped through Delhi's late-night streets, his fingers flew over his phone, booking the flight that could make or break his plan.

Minutes later, the taxi stopped outside his bungalow. Arjan slipped inside silently, careful not to stir his family. Moving quickly, he grabbed his passport, phone charger, and a few clothes. With a final glance around, he steeled himself with thoughts of Sahin – the reason for this madness – and stepped back outside, duffel bag in hand. Locking the door behind him, he hurried back to the cab. As he slid into the back seat, he pulled out his phone and dialled Faiz.

"Faiz," he began, his voice urgent. "Did you see the article Zafar posted?"

"I'm on it," Faiz replied.

"Is Sahin one of them?" Arjan's grip tightened on the phone.

"It's the sniper unit," Faiz said cautiously. "But about Sahin… I'm not sure. They haven't released any capture video yet."

"God!" Arjan muttered, his voice shaking. "I'm leaving for Sulaymaniyah right now."

"What?" Faiz's voice rose sharply. "Have you lost your mind? What's your plan? Don't be rash – use your head."

Arjan's cheeks burned, irritation flaring at the all-too-familiar tone. He'd heard it before – from his father, from squad mates, from Priya; from anyone who'd doubted his judgement.

"You know what?" Arjan said, his voice hardening. "I don't care. If I were in trouble, Sahin would come for me, just like she always did. She wouldn't sit around and wait for me to die. So, I'm going to find a way to get to her, come what may!"

"Arjan," Faiz shot back, exasperated. "Don't mix virtual heroics with real life. It doesn't work like that! You'll just end up getting killed."

"Remember our motto? No Ace Left Behind. What's it worth if we don't live by it?" Arjan countered.

"It's not a game. You're talking about throwing yourself into a real-life war zone!" Faiz said firmly. But then his voice softened, a note of pleading breaking through. "I get it, I respect your feelings, but you need a plan. Don't just rush in blind!"

"Plans have only wasted time," Arjan said. "And time is something Sahin doesn't have. I can't wait any longer!"

A long pause stretched between them before Faiz spoke again, his tone heavy. "What are you going to do, Arjan? How do you think you're going to save her?"

"I'll figure it out," Arjan replied. "I'm not trying to be a hero. I just want to honour my love and stand by her at a time when she needs me the most. That's all."

Faiz sighed deeply; his resignation clear. "For God's sake, keep your head down and stay safe."

"I will. Hope always," Arjan said softly.

"Hope always," Faiz echoed.

As the taxi pulled up to the bustling departure terminal, Arjan ended the call, and stepped into the chaos.

Every step toward the plane tightened the knot in his stomach. At the boarding area, his mind raced – was he prepared for what lay ahead? He felt like a criminal on the run. This wasn't him; the most rebellious thing he'd ever done was bunk school. And now, he was defying not just parental expectations, but international law.

Seated by the aircraft window, he stowed his bag and leaned back, closing his eyes. He let out a deep breath, trying to steady the storm of emotions within him. His thoughts lingered on Sahin – her fate, their uncertain future, and the dangerous path ahead.

As the aircraft lifted off the tarmac, Arjan pressed his forehead against the cool window, watching dawn break over the horizon. This was his leap of faith – his flight into the unknown. Below, the familiar landscape of his homeland receded into the distance. There was no turning back now.

11
Red Notice

The aircraft descended smoothly through clear skies over Iraq, landing gently on the runway. The screech of tires on the tarmac jolted Arjan awake. Blinking away the remnants of sleep, he caught the flight crew's announcement: "We hope you have a pleasant stay. Thank you for choosing Air Arab."

Arjan took a moment to gather his surroundings as the weight of his mission came rushing back. Around him, the dimming seatbelt sign triggered a symphony of metal clicks and the rustle of passengers stretching and retrieving their belongings. Remaining seated, Arjan gazed out the window at the modest terminal of Sulaymaniyah International Airport. Its name, emblazoned in bold green letters on a stark white facade, offered a quiet welcome to this less frequented gateway. Nestled in the eastern stretches of Iraqi Kurdistan, Sulaymaniyah stood as a haven within the autonomous Kurdish region – a rare enclave of relative safety and political stability. It had become a sanctuary for Kurdish sympathizers and others seeking refuge from the relentless regional turmoil.

Stepping onto the tarmac, Arjan was greeted by the mild, dust-laden air as he headed toward the small, bustling terminal. Inside, he joined the slow-moving queue at immigration, each step toward the counter amplifying his anxiety. His fate hinged on a single hope – that the intelligence agency hadn't caught on to his escape. Or worse, that a Red Notice hadn't been issued yet. Yes, a Red Notice – when your country enlists Interpol to track you down. From gamer to fugitive, things had escalated rather quickly.

When his turn came, Arjan stepped up to the immigration counter, trying to project calm. The officer, a stern-faced man with a discernible Syrian accent, scrutinized him as he handed over his documents. With deliberate precision, the officer flipped through the passport pages, his expression giving nothing away.

"What brings you to Sulaymaniyah, Mr Arjan?" he asked in a tone that felt like an interrogation to Arjan.

"I'm visiting a friend," Arjan replied, his voice steadier than he felt.

"And where does this friend live?"

"In Sulaymaniyah," Arjan said, masking his nervousness.

"When are you planning to return to India?"

"In about a week," Arjan answered, hoping the brevity would dispel any suspicion.

"Are you travelling alone?"

"Yes," Arjan replied quickly.

"May I see your return ticket?" the officer asked, fixing him with an intent gaze.

Arjan froze. Fumbling with his phone, he pretended to search for the digital proof that did not exist.

Before he could think of an excuse, a senior officer approached, murmuring discreetly into the first officer's ear. Arjan's pulse thundered in his ears, his nerves taut as he watched their quiet deliberation. This didn't feel routine. He bit his lip, the tang of fear sharp in his mouth as he braced himself for the worst.

The first officer, now stroking his chin beard thoughtfully, picked up Arjan's passport and flipped it open again.

"Mr Arjan, you do realize your country has issued a…" he began, his tone grave.

Arjan's face drained of colour. "Issued a what?" he stammered, panic creeping into his voice.

The officer frowned. "Would you let me finish?"

"I'm sorry," Arjan blurted quickly.

"India has issued a travel advisory for our country," the officer said flatly.

Arjan exhaled a shaky breath of relief. "Oh! Yes, I am aware of that."

"And your family – are they aware of your visit here?"

"Yes, they know," Arjan responded.

The officer held Arjan in an unblinking stare, as if weighing his sincerity. Arjan felt ready to crumble under the scrutiny. But then, without a word, the officer stamped his passport briskly and called out, "Next!"

Arjan snatched up his passport and hurried toward the exit, relief washing over him with each step away from the counter.

As Arjan stepped out of the airport, he was glued to a travel guide app on his phone, navigating his way through the crowd that swarmed outside the terminal. His eyes caught a decrepit kiosk near the exit, bearing the insignia of a Kurdish faction. It was a modest setup: an open stall with a thin canvas frame and a lone wooden desk. Posters of Kurdish women fighters, armed and poised, adorned the flimsy walls, lending a stern atmosphere.

Peering into the empty booth for a closer look, Arjan was startled when a thick-bearded man in his thirties approached briskly from a distance. "Good morning! I am Abdul. Welcome to Sulaymaniyah," he greeted warmly.

"Hi, I'm Arjan from India," Arjan replied cautiously.

"Yes, yes, we received your papers last night," Abdul said with a nod. "We were expecting you."

"Oh! Okay," Arjan responded.

"Where is your luggage?" Abdul inquired, scanning the area.

"There," Arjan said, pointing to his duffel bag.

"That's it? You travel light, eh?" Abdul chuckled.

Arjan forced a faint smile. Despite Abdul's hospitable demeanor, Arjan couldn't shake off the skepticism. He'd read reports of foreign nationals kidnapped by ISIS men posing as Kurdish recruiters. The danger felt real. It was nearly impossible for Arjan to tell them apart.

Abdul led him to a grey Hyundai Santa Fe. After popping the trunk, he gestured for Arjan to load his bag. Arjan paused, surveying the parking lot with heightened alertness, before sliding into the back seat.

Inside, he was startled to find three other passengers, their curious eyes sizing him up. The silence hung awkwardly until Abdul spoke. "Guys, this is Arjan from India. Like you, he's a recruit in the great resistance."

The engine rumbled to life, and the vehicle began its journey.

"Hi!" Arjan said sheepishly.

"He's Ron, from Birmingham," Abdul said, nodding toward a plump, freckled Caucasian man. "That's Ahmed, from London," he continued, motioning to a hefty, bearded man in the front seat. "And that's Jamie, also from London," he finished, indicating a wiry man with bushy eyebrows and glasses.

Each of the Britons offered an awkward smile, which Arjan returned with a polite nod. As the car pulled away from the airport, Arjan wrestled with his thoughts. Was he being paranoid? The presence of other foreigners in similar circumstances should have been reassuring, yet it only intensified his fears.

* * *

ISIS may have been a billion-dollar organization, but its greatest asset lay in the flinty allegiance and unwavering fidelity of its fighters. Its ability to lure foreigners into its blood-soaked ranks was particularly concerning, with Britons making up the largest foreign contingent – nearly 900 had joined ISIS. For many of these recruits, Islam or the vision of a Caliphate had little to do with their decision to join. Alienated from their own societies, they were highly susceptible to latching onto alternative ideologies. Some sought escape from personal struggles, others were lured by promises of money or the thrill of adventure amidst violence, and a few craved a sense of purpose or self-worth that eluded them in their home countries. Within ISIS, foreign fighters faced stark disparities. South Asians were considered weak and frequently manipulated into suicide missions. Yet, they continued to join in significant numbers each month.

This phenomenon gave ISIS the ability to extend its influence far beyond its controlled territories. Foreign fighters carried with them both battlefield experience and extremist indoctrination, and the prospect of these individuals slipping back into their home countries posed a serious threat to global security.

★ ★ ★

Under the pale moonlight, the tires of the Hyundai SUV crunched over gravel, coming to a stop in front of a rundown building in Al-Qanat, a ghost town on the fringes of the Iraq-Syrian border. The headlights swept over the façade, revealing peeling paint and boarded-up windows, before the light cut out, leaving the weak, erratic flicker of a streetlamp to pierce the darkness. As the engine died, a heavy silence enveloped the group.

Abdul turned to his passengers, announcing, "Guys! We've reached the safe house."

Met with no response, he glanced back at the sleeping recruits. Clearing his throat, he called louder, his hoarse voice cutting through the quiet. "Hello!"

The sharp sound jolted the passengers awake.

Arjan sat up abruptly, his head spinning slightly – a lingering effect of the red-eye flight and grueling eight-hour road trip. Rubbing his eyes, he peered through the dusty window at the shadowy structure.

One by one, the recruits clambered out of the SUV, stretching their stiff limbs and squinting into the darkness. They unloaded their bags and trudged toward the decrepit building that stood isolated in the middle of nowhere.

As Abdul led them inside, he gave a quick tour of the makeshift safe house. It was an abandoned primary school. Most rooms were vacant, save for a few tiny chairs shoved into corners. Torn hand-drawn sketches and faded paintings clung to the cracked walls, haunting remnants of a happier past. Arjan was visibly unsettled by the surroundings; he covered his face with his hand to ward off the dust and the musty, rancid smell that filled the air.

"This place isn't much, but it's safe," Abdul reassured them. "We'll be staying here overnight and cross into Syria tomorrow."

As they moved to the next room, Arjan felt the familiar tickle of dust irritating his nose. Frantically patting his pockets for his nasal spray, he realized it wasn't there. With a groan, he rummaged through his duffel bag only to confirm his fear – his trusty spray had been left behind.

Abdul led them into what had once been a classroom, now stripped of its original purpose. "This is where you'll be briefed tomorrow before we head out," he said as the floorboards creaked beneath him. He flicked the switch, but the tube light only sputtered weakly before dying. "No matter," he shrugged, "we won't need it."

The room, repurposed for training, contained little more than a chalkboard and a few scattered chairs. The rough, unpainted walls displayed the Kurdish flag alongside posters of fighters, their faces beginning to feel vaguely familiar, standing out against the room's decay.

Next, Abdul ushered them into an adjacent room with a few old, tattered mattresses strewn across the floor. Their frayed edges and thin padding promised little comfort. Arjan scanned the communal sleep area with a stoic expression. He hadn't quite expected royalty, of course, he had tempered his expectations. But even so, the harsh reality of the place hit him harder than he anticipated.

"This is where you'll sleep," Abdul said. "There's food and water in the pantry, so help yourselves. Any questions?" He scanned the recruits as they placed their bags in a corner and claimed spots on the mattresses.

Arjan, struggling with rising discomfort, hesitated before asking, his voice nasally from congestion, "Is there a chance I could find some Otrivin spray?"

The recruits exchanged puzzled glances, and Abdul, pulling out a notepad and pen, feigned making a list. "Would you also like a Big Mac from McDonald's?" he quipped, a smirk tugging at his lips.

Arjan squinted at Abdul, unsure if it was meant as a joke.

Ron, picking up on the humour, chimed in, "Might as well throw in some fries and a soda to make it a Happy Meal, eh?"

Laughter erupted, but seeing Arjan's mortified expression, Abdul quickly softened. "Sorry, I couldn't resist," he said sincerely. "The nearest pharmacy is about a hundred kilometres away. That's why I asked earlier if anyone needed anything."

Arjan nodded, resigned to the situation.

Jamie stepped closer and whispered, "Don't worry, mate. My grandma taught me a few tricks for blocked noses. I'll help you out."

Arjan managed a weak smile, grateful for the gesture.

Abdul clapped his hands to regain everyone's attention. "Alright, then. Get some rest. Tomorrow, we'll need all the focus and strength you've got. I'll see you in the morning."

* * *

Later that night, Arjan sat alone on a rickety wooden chair in the open verandah, gazing at the night sky. The cold air made his blocked nose sniffle, and the moonlight cast shadows on his face, reflecting the storm of emotions within. Lost in thought, he pulled out his iPhone, his fingers trembling slightly as he scrolled to 'Papa'. His thumb hovered over the call button, hesitation gripping him, before he slipped the phone back into his pocket, unable to summon the courage. Moments later, a surge of resolve overtook him. He pulled the phone out again and hit call before doubt could hold him back. As the phone rang, his breath quickened.

Rajesh stirred awake at the sound of his phone vibrating on the bedside table. He sat up instantly, reaching for it as if he'd been subconsciously waiting for this moment. Beside him, Anita blinked awake, her wide, worried eyes meeting his.

"Is it Arjan?" she asked anxiously.

Pressing the phone to his ear, Rajesh nodded, his voice tight with anticipation. "Hello?"

"Hello, Papa," Arjan mumbled, rising from his chair at the sound of his father's voice.

"Arjan! Where have you been? We've been so worried," Rajesh's voice cracked with emotion.

"I'm fine, Papa," Arjan tried to reassure him, though his voice quavered.

"Your phone was unreachable. You should have at least left a message!"

"I'm sorry, Papa."

"Where are you?" Rajesh's tone grew urgent.

Summoning his courage, Arjan replied, "Papa, I'm in Iraq."

A heavy silence fell over the line.

"This is not the time for jokes," Rajesh said finally, disbelief in his voice.

"Papa, I'm telling the truth," Arjan admitted.

Hearing his son's tone, Rajesh realized he wasn't joking. "What the hell are you doing in Iraq? How did you even get there? There's a war going on!" His words tumbled out in frantic shock.

Anita's alarm spiked as she overheard the conversation. "Iraq? What is he saying?" she asked Rajesh, panic in her voice.

"Papa, I'm going to Syria now. My girlfriend is trapped there. I have to save her," Arjan confessed, his voice firm but heavy with emotion.

"What is going on? Are you in your senses?" Rajesh roared, his desperation boiling over. "This is madness! Do you understand how dangerous this is?"

Anita, now on the verge of tears, clutched at Rajesh's arm.

"Papa, I'm sorry for putting you through this," Arjan pleaded. "I had no choice. If I make it back, I'll explain everything."

"Tell me this isn't true. Please, Arjan, stop this madness!" Rajesh's voice cracked, tears choking his words.

Unable to endure the silence that followed, Anita grabbed the phone. "Arjan, where are you? Are you safe?" she asked, her voice racked with emotion.

"I'm so sorry, Mumma," Arjan sobbed. "I know I've let you both down. Please forgive me. I'm a terrible son."

Hearing their son's confession, Anita and Rajesh broke down. The heart-wrenching sound of his parents crying – a stark realization of the pain he had inflicted – left Arjan with a searing ache in his chest. His own tears blurred his vision, and a lump swelled in his throat. Unable to endure it any longer, he quietly ended the call. The phone slipped from his trembling hands as he collapsed back into the chair, burying his face in his palms.

Tormented by remorse, Arjan questioned the worth of his decision. He knew he had failed his parents. For what? He had no guarantee he could even cross into Syria. He had come this far for Sahin, but did she even survive? Over a week had passed since that news clip featuring Sahin aired. Every day, ISIS captured and executed Kurdish fighters. Even if she was alive, how could he find her in a war-torn country, let alone rescue her?

Lost in grief, Arjan froze at the faint sound of footsteps approaching. Hastily wiping his tears, he tried to conceal his vulnerability. Jamie appeared beside him, resting a reassuring hand on his shoulder. "Be strong, my friend. Should I get you some water?" he asked, his voice gentle yet firm.

Arjan cleared his throat, keeping his head low. "I'm okay," he murmured.

Jamie pulled up a chair and sat beside him. As silence settled between them, Arjan scratched his forehead, an unconscious attempt to mask his face and emotions.

"Come on. There's no shame in crying. Men cry too," Jamie said. "If I may ask, is it about your girlfriend?"

"No," Arjan muttered, lifting his head and wiping away the remnants of tears with the back of his hand. "My parents."

"You told them where you are?"

Arjan nodded, his expression sombre.

"I can imagine. It's not easy, and it takes guts to do what you did," Jamie said with quiet empathy.

Arjan stayed silent, lost in thought.

"Do you want to go back?" Jamie asked.

Arjan hesitated, then sighed. "I'm afraid it's not going to be that simple, even if I wanted to."

Jamie frowned slightly. "What? You're wanted there or something?" he asked with a chuckle, trying to ease the tension.

"That's… actually not a bad guess," Arjan replied.

"Really? I was just trying to be funny," Jamie said, taken aback.

"I didn't even get to say goodbye to my parents," Arjan mumbled.

There was a pause as Arjan and Jamie exchanged sympathetic looks.

"Could you say goodbye to yours?" Arjan asked hesitantly.

"No," Jamie replied, adjusting his glasses. "There's no one at home. There's no home. My parents died when I was seven."

"Oh. I'm sorry," Arjan said, leaning forward, his compassion evident.

"Come on, spare me the waterworks," Jamie waved off the concern with a half-smile. "I'll make my parents proud and meet them soon in Jannah."

Arjan listened, moved by Jamie's grit and conviction.

"Not many have the courage to join a holy resistance," Jamie continued, his voice fiery. "We're part of a revolution. We'll be in the history books."

Arjan nodded, feeling a flicker of determination light within him.

"Now cheer up, mate. My brother from another mother," Jamie said, offering a reassuring smile.

Arjan managed a faint smile in return.

"There you go. Now that you're smiling, tell me your story."

"Let it be. It's a long one," Arjan muttered, reluctant to open up.

"I've got all the time in the world," Jamie insisted, eager to strengthen their bond.

As the night deepened, the two talked, their camaraderie growing. They had quickly hit it off, just like people do in battle zones where shared dangers forge fast friendships.

12
Game Over

Having pledged their allegiance to the Kurdish resistance, Arjan and his fellow recruits set out on their mission to cross into Syria. Under the thick veil of darkness, Abdul dropped them off near the border, where the most treacherous part of their journey awaited. The Iraqi Syrian border was infamous as one of the world's deadliest – a minefield littered with IEDs. An abandoned toy or a seemingly innocuous piece of scrap metal could be riddled with a detonator. With ISIS fighters patrolling the area, the stakes were very high; capture would mean certain death. They were warned not to speak to anyone, as ISIS spies could be lurking anywhere.

For the most formidable mission of their lives, they received no formal training or detailed briefing. Instead, they were handed a haphazard collection of hazard warnings, delivered with the unnerving casualness of passing a grocery list – except this list was for navigating a war zone. Without so much as a tutorial, they felt thrust into a video game set to its hardest difficulty. But in this grim reality, a single mistake meant permadeath.

Their mission objectives were clear:

Cross into Syrian territory undetected before dawn

Locate and board the truck arranged by a Syrian contact

Conceal themselves among the cargo and avoid detection during the journey

Successfully unite with the Kurdish resistance in Kobani

Clad in camouflage, with hearts pounding, the recruits set off on foot. They crept through the shadowy borderlands, senses heightened to catch the faintest sound or movement. Every step risked triggering an explosive; every shadow hinted at danger. Guided only by primal instincts and Abdul's stern warnings, their survival teetered on a knife's edge. Each rustle of wind and crackle of dry leaves amplified the tension, turning their trek into a deadly game of endurance.

After an exhausting five-mile trek, they reached the designated meeting point – an abandoned construction site where a rusted truck was hidden from view. The sight of it brought a fleeting sense of relief. They had crossed into Syria unscathed. A man with a weathered face emerged from behind the truck, his voice low and urgent. "Quickly, before the sun rises," he ordered, his tone sharp. As they approached, the back of the truck swung open, revealing a cramped, grimy interior filled with livestock. The recruits clambered into the truck bed, wedging themselves between cages and sacks of feed, trying to blend into the surroundings. As the truck rumbled through the desert, hot air seeped through the tarp slits, mixing with the pungent stench of animals and fodder.

With each passing kilometre, they penetrated deeper into hostile territory. The stakes grew higher, the margin for error vanished, and the anticipation of reaching Kobani weighed heavily on their minds. Hope flickered and faded with every breath, as their journey hurtled them closer to the unknown.

Moments later, the truck approached a heavily manned checkpoint, and the driver's face turned pale as two armed militants flagged them down. The truck lurched to a stop. His voice trembled as he spoke quickly, desperately trying to reason with them, but his pleas meant nothing. In an instant, he was yanked from the seat and shoved aside.

A cold-eyed, bearded militant barked orders, his rifle pointed menacingly. Under duress, the driver raised his hands and weakly gestured toward the back of the truck. The militants wasted no time, surrounding the vehicle and forcing open the rear door.

The recruits found themselves plunged into their worst nightmare. The sudden intrusion sent the cattle into a frenzied stampede, adding to the chaos. Militants with AK-47s slung over their shoulders violently dragged the recruits by their hair.

Jamie refused to surrender. His fiery defiance cut through the tension as he argued in broken Arabic, desperately repeating, *"'Astatie 'an 'ashrah. 'Astatie 'an 'ashrah."*

While he protested, his right hand slipped into his jacket – a move that instantly alarmed the gunmen. One reacted swiftly, slamming the rifle butt into Jamie's abdomen, sending him crumpling to the ground in agony.

"Hamza will take care of this one," the burly militant ordered. "Take the others to the site. Shoot anyone who resists."

As Jamie was hauled away, his shattered spectacles lay abandoned on the dirt road. Arjan stifled a cry, helpless against his friend's suffering. Moments later, he, Ron, and Ahmed were blindfolded and handcuffed, their feeble struggles crushed by the militants' brute force.

Shoved into the backseat of an SUV, Arjan couldn't shake the haunting image of Jamie's final act of defiance. While the rest had surrendered meekly, Jamie had fought back, staring death in the face. Whether it was heroic or simply suicidal, Arjan couldn't tell. In the end, it didn't seem to matter – ISIS would kill them all, resistance or not.

As the SUV pulled away, gunshots rang out behind them, echoing across the desert. The militants sneered cruelly.

"That must be your friend," one taunted.

"Don't worry. You'll meet him soon, in hell!" another added with a sadistic grin.

Forced into the brace position, the recruits squirmed, overwhelmed by fear, pain, and the chilling certainty of a grim fate.

* * *

Present Day

The SUV screeched to a halt in the barren desert, throwing up clouds of dust. The recruits were dragged out and marched toward a makeshift execution site. Through his frayed blindfold, Arjan caught glimpses of the surroundings.

A high-definition camera stood ready to capture the execution, and a massive green screen loomed behind it, masking the true location. Nearby, an open grave overflowed with bodies, many of them female fighters in fatigues identical to the ones Sahin wore in the news footage. Arjan's heart seized in terror. "Sahin! Sahin!" he cried at the horrific sight, his voice breaking.

A militant struck him with a brutal kick, driving him to his knees. "Cooperate, or I'll make it slow and painful," the man growled. Arjan, gasping for breath, fell silent. Beside him, Ron and Ahmed were thrown to the ground, their bodies hitting the sunbaked earth with a dull thud.

Six militants dressed in black garbs and balaclavas moved into position. One waved a black flag while another adjusted the camcorder, ensuring the scene would be filmed in all its gruesome detail.

"Allahu Akbar!" The fervent chants pierced the eerie silence as the militiamen took positions behind the captives, assault rifles in hand. Arjan could feel his heart slamming against his ribcage. Without warning, the executioners opened fire. The Kalashnikovs roared, bullets tearing into the sky and spewing acrid smoke as spent casings clattered to the ground. Amidst the tumult, the militiamen jeered raucously at the trembling captives.

Unamused by the theatrics, Hamza, the bespectacled field commander with hooded brown eyes and a stocky frame, raised his hand. His silent command carried a weight that instantly restored solemnity to the grim proceedings.

The militiamen fell back into formation, reloading their weapons with sharp metallic clinks that rang out in the tension-laden air. For the captives, the agonizing wait felt endless. Beneath his blindfold, Arjan squeezed his eyes shut and murmured a prayer.

The thugs raised their rifles again, fingers hovering over the triggers as they awaited the cameraman's signal.

"Spread out a little. You don't want a bloodbath, do you?" the cameraman barked, visibly underwhelmed by the mise-en-scène.

The executioners grabbed the captives by the scruff of their necks, roughly repositioning them about four feet apart.

The cameraman peered through the viewfinder, signaling his approval with a brisk thumbs-up. "Mashallah," he muttered.

Arjan's heartbeat quickened as the muzzle of an assault rifle pressed against the back of his head.

The cameraman punched the record button and called out, "Rolling."

A profound sense of dread overcame the captives, who, in that chilling moment, let go of their souls.

"Who's up first?" the cameraman asked, seeking to fine-tune his focus.

"Let's keep it a surprise… who's it gonna be?" a voice replied, tinged with a disturbing sense of schadenfreude.

"It's like Russian roulette," another jeered, "Except all of you die."

Laughter erupted among the militiamen, abruptly punctuated by a gunshot. Arjan's heart skipped a beat. With a sickening thud, Ahmed's lifeless body crumpled to the parched ground, blood pooling beneath him. Arjan and Ron, numb with dread, could no longer bear the anticipation.

On his turn, Arjan's executioner cocked his rifle, the sharp click slicing though the tension like a blade. Bracing for the inevitable, Arjan clenched his fists and gritted his teeth, every muscle in his body taut with fear. The executioner pulled the trigger halfway when—

BOOM!

A thunderous blast ripped through the dunes, shattering the scene into chaos before everything dissolved into darkness.

13
Ludonarrative Dissonance

Arjan lay flat on his back, his limbs sprawled carelessly like the spokes of a broken wheel. He was enveloped in an overwhelming sensation of weightlessness, as if his body had transcended the earthly bounds and floated amongst the clouds. The stratospheric breeze caressed him gently, fluttering across his skin with the softness of a whisper. Around him, complete silence held sway, paired with an all-consuming darkness that seemed to stretch into infinity. It was as if time itself had come to a standstill, letting him drift in this boundless void, far, far away from the world.

Just then, a faint, distant rumbling began to disturb the eternal silence, sending gentle ripples across his body. These ripples gradually intensified as the sound grew nearer and less gentle, escalating until the ripples morphed into tides and the noise into a thunderous staccato of drumbeats. Arjan's eyelids fluttered open. His senses stirred, reporting back to a mind that was struggling to understand. Then, a salvo of gunshots ripped through the air. The menacing roar engulfed him. Startled, he jolted upright. His eyes darted around wildly, unable to piece together his surroundings. He was not on a battlefield nor nestled among heavenly clouds; instead, he lay on a cot inside a tarpaulin tent. Glancing down, he ran his hands over his body in disbelief. Alive. He was alive. Rising unsteadily, he caught sight of his reflection in a small, cracked mirror. His skin bore bruises from handcuffs and the rough grip of ISIS mercenaries, but he was whole. Unshackled.

Another burst of gunfire shattered the stillness; adrenaline coursed through his veins. A sliver of sunlight pierced the tent through a small tear, catching his eye. With trembling fingers, he pulled back the tarp, desperate for a clue to his whereabouts. Outside, a cohort of fighters practiced their marksmanship, while nearby, a cluster of women assembled their weapons. As he looked at their faces, one among them was none other than Sahin's. Was he still dreaming? His eyes widened. Was it really her or just a mirage conjured by his frantic mind? As he stared, there was no mistaking it. Sahin sat on an overturned crate, her commanding presence undeniable as she wrapped her sniper rifle in camo tape.

Arjan froze, his breath hitching at the sight of her. Overcome with emotion, he bolted out of the tent, arms flailing and cries of relief spilling from his lips. "Sahin! Sahin!"

At the sound of his voice, Sahin stood up abruptly. She turned just as he reached her, pulling her into a tight embrace. Her body stiffened in his arms. Relief flickered across her features but was quickly masked by a guarded expression. The public display of affection made her uneasy, aware of the curious glances from her fellow fighters.

Arjan's voice cracked under the weight of his emotions. "Is this real? Oh my God, I can't believe it!" His words spilled out, raw and unfiltered. Tears of joy streaked his face as he continued, "I'm so relieved you're safe. I… I can't believe it's really you, Sahin! I thought I had lost you forever."

Sahin met his tearful gaze with empathetic eyes, her own emotions threatening to surface, but the darting gazes around her snapped her back to control. Her jaw tightened as she swallowed the lump rising in her throat. She couldn't allow herself to look fragile.

Arjan, oblivious to her inner turmoil, began to speak in a frantic rush. "Thinking about it now, I can't believe I'm alive either. What happened? How did I end up here? I can't believe you are standing in front of me. You won't believe what I felt when I got the news of your town falling. I was anxious to get to you!" His words tumbled out faster than he could control.

Sahin shifted her weight, subtly stepping back to create a hint of distance. Her voice, low and measured, carried a whisper of genuine concern. "How are you feeling now? Are you hurt?" she asked, the urgency in her tone muted but undeniable.

"I'm okay, but I don't remember anything. I was about to be executed, then a bomb went off, and everything went dark. I thought it was game over… I don't know what happened. How we got out of there… who rescued us…" Arjan replied, his voice tinged with lingering shock.

"I know. It was my team that intervened," Sahin confirmed.

"Really? So, those jihadists are gone?"

"Yes, we took them out," Sahin stated, her voice taking on a formal edge.

Arjan's eyes widened. "Oh my God! You rescued me for real, just like you always did in games."

Sahin gave a brief nod, though the comparison drew a flicker of impatience.

"Wait," Arjan said, his brows furrowing as he scrutinized himself. "I was right in the thick of it. How did I escape unscathed?"

"They weren't frag grenades," Sahin explained. "It was a coordinated operation. Allied jets dropped flashbangs to disorient the captors while we neutralized them with sniper fire."

"Wow! But how did you even know I was there?" Arjan pressed, his curiosity deepening.

"I didn't," Sahin replied flatly.

Arjan blinked, his confusion evident.

"We received intel that our captured women fighters were being taken there for execution," Sahin continued, her tone heavier now. "We worked with the Americans, hoping to rescue them. Sadly, we…"

Arjan leaned in eagerly, cutting her off. "A joint op! How slick – it's just like that mission in—"

Sahin's patience frayed. "Arjan! This is real war. The bullets are real, the wounds fester, and the deaths are permanent. When you die, there are no respawns. When an ally falls, you don't just rage-quit; you carry their body back, you bury them, and sometimes, you must look into the eyes of their grieving families, if they have any left. This is nothing like a video game, for God's sake."

Her words struck with the force of a freight train, and Arjan recoiled slightly, startled by the intensity.

She sighed, the weight of her grief pressing down on her. "I lost five of my sisters in this mission. I couldn't save them."

"Hey, I'm sorry," Arjan said quickly. "I didn't mean to sound insensitive. I know it's serious – I've been through a lot too, you know."

Sahin's eyes stayed cold, narrowing slightly as his words hung in the air.

"Look, Sahin, I've already lost two friends on this journey. I nearly died out there – for you."

"For me?" Sahin's voice rose, incredulous. "I never asked you to come here, Arjan. How did you even get here?"

"What's the matter with you?" Arjan said, frustration flaring. "I thought you'd be happy to see me. I travelled all this way to find you."

Sahin's gaze faltered, guilt flickering briefly. Arjan's arrival and now his life now in her hands felt like a fragile treasure in her crumbling world. Every day, people were dying, and the thought of him becoming one of them terrified her.

"This isn't your fight, Arjan," she said. "You shouldn't have risked your life."

"But I love you, Sahin. How could I leave you to face all this alone? All I could think about was getting to you."

"You don't have to throw your life away like this," Sahin urged, her tone softening as she tried to make him see reason. "Think of your parents. They must be worried sick."

"I'm not going anywhere without you," Arjan replied resolutely.

"And I cannot abandon my people and flee," Sahin said, her tone steely. Yet beneath her conviction, his devotion tugged at her, even as it sparked quiet frustration.

"And what about us?" Arjan asked, his voice laced with desperation. "Does that mean nothing to you?"

"It meant something once," Sahin said, her voice low, almost breaking. "But that feels like another life. I've seen too much – watched my people massacred in front of me. Avenging them is the only thing on my mind."

"Then I'm staying too," Arjan said firmly. "I'll stand by you. No matter what."

Sahin shook her head, exasperation etched into her features. "Why don't you understand? We're running out of fighters, weapons – everything. We don't expect to survive this war. It's a suicide mission. Let me arrange for your safe exit before it's too late."

"I'm not leaving, Sahin."

"What will you even do here? You have no experience in war. You'll only get yourself killed!"

"I'll learn. My decision is final. I'm not going anywhere, Sahin. You mean the world to me. And I will be by your side come what may!"

Sahin's hand trembled before she clenched it at her side. "We can't afford distractions, Arjan. I can't afford them. Not when my people are counting on me." Her voice quavered for a moment, then hardened. "You won't listen to me? Fine. Stay if you must but stay out of my way. I can't be weak, not now."

She turned abruptly, her steps firm, leaving Arjan standing alone, the weight of her words sinking deep.

★ ★ ★

Arjan stared at his reflection in the cracked mirror, tugging at the fabric of his camouflage fatigues hanging from his lean frame. The uniform, a size too big, made him feel as if he were trying to fill boots much bigger than his own. Perhaps it wasn't just the uniform – it was the promise to join the resistance, a commitment spurred more by his longing to stand beside Sahin than by belief in the cause.

Sahin, consumed with far graver concerns, had no space to rekindle a love that had faded on her end. Was he deluding himself, hoping to win her back by joining her fight? Doubts gnawed at him. Was his pledge too impulsive, too coloured by personal desires? Was he trying too hard to prove he could survive the trials of war?

Taking a deep breath, Arjan stepped into the brisk morning air. His boots thudded softly against the barren ground as he made his way to the training area. Ahead, an abandoned community complex loomed – a once-thriving hub now repurposed as the operational heart of the Kurdish resistance. The two-story building, crumbling and in shambles, was fortified by a high boundary wall. Its facade, scarred with the marks of battle, echoed stories of past skirmishes and ongoing struggles. Rudimentary guard towers, constructed from rusted iron, cast long shadows across the base. These towers served dual purposes as sniper posts and watch points, crucial for the stronghold's defence.

As he moved through the compound, he passed a desolate corner that housed a forgotten children's play area, where rusty swings and seesaws creaked mournfully with each gust of wind. A stone's throw away, a small armory depot displayed neatly stacked weapons and crates of ammunition. Nearby, a turret gun, positioned by a sandbag bunker, stood as a silent guardian. Further along, the schoolyard-turned-bootcamp, buzzed with the energy of about sixty fighters congregating, the majority being young women, with only a handful of men scattered among them. At the edge of the field, an ancient olive tree spread its gnarled branches wide, its enduring presence a quiet witness to the struggles and resilience of the fighters who sought its shade.

Awira, the regiment's commanding officer, strode onto the field, her imposing presence demanding instant attention. "Gather round," she called, her voice resonant and firm, slicing through the morning hubbub. The fighters snapped to attention, clustering around her.

In her hands, Awira held two military trucker caps, symbols of tradition and a rite of passage into their ranks. "Arjan, Ron!" she called, beckoning them forward.

The crowd parted like water, clearing a path for the two newcomers. As Arjan stepped closer, he felt the weight of sharp, evaluating gazes from the fighters around him.

Awira held the cap before Arjan, pausing briefly. "Welcome to Rojava," she said, placing the cap firmly on his head. "You're part of the great resistance now."

The cap fit snugly, a welcome change from his loose uniform. A swell of pride rose in Arjan, not just from joining but from a deep sense of belonging. On the edge of the gathering, Sahin watched in silence, her expression unreadable. For a fleeting moment, their eyes met, a swirl of unspoken emotions passing between them.

As Awira bestowed the same honour upon Ron, the gravity of the moment deepened. "You've now transformed from civilians to defenders of the Kurdish cause," she declared. The air erupted with war cries and slogans, a resounding welcome from their comrades. Despite the grim reality, the sense of camaraderie and shared purpose was undeniable.

A short distance away, two fighters stationed at the base entrance observed the ceremony. Zoran, towering and built like a tank, hoisted a heavy sandbag for shoulder presses, his keen eyes sizing up Arjan. Beside him, Asos, broad and stocky, leaned against the gun turret, puffing on a cigarette.

Wiping sweat from his brow, Zoran grumbled in Kurdish, "What's with the recruits getting worse with every batch? Where did they get those guys from?"

Asos took a slow drag, nodding toward Arjan. "The softie is Sahin's friend from some online game – part of her squad or something. He's from India,"

"A lover boy then?" Zoran's tone mixed amusement with scorn.

"What do you mean?" Asos raised an eyebrow.

"He's come to Kobani for her. What else can drive you this crazy?" Zoran scoffed, motioning for the cigarette.

Asos chuckled, a wry smile playing on his lips as he passed the cigarette, "The things love makes you do."

Taking a deep drag, Zoran exhaled slowly, the smoke curling around his words, "So now we're taking in every Tom, Dick, and Harry who shows up? To fight the enemy with the likes of these…"

Nearby, Nasrin, a spirited teenage fighter, applied vibrant strokes to a graffiti depiction of the Kurdistan flag on the boundary wall. Overhearing their conversation, she paused and turned toward them, spray can in hand. "Never judge a book by its cover," she said. "You haven't seen him in action yet. Who knows how good he is. After all, he made it all the way here, didn't he?"

Zoran remarked, "I can tell a lot about a fighter just by looking. I bet you a hundred liras that he's never even thrown a punch in school. Fighting online battles is not the same, let me tell you."

Nasrin shook the spray can, the clinking of the mixing ball inside resonating briefly, before she aimed it at the wall. "We're short of fighters, you know that. If I were Awira, I'd welcome anyone committed to the cause with open arms."

"You think a ragtag bunch of misfits will win this war?" Zoran asked skeptically.

She added a bold stroke of green to the wall, turning back with conviction, "You never know. Every fighter brings their own destiny."

"You're too naive," Zoran muttered, the smoke from his cigarette weaving through the dusty air.

"You're too judgmental," Nasrin countered smoothly, her gaze steady.

"Don't argue, man," Asos interjected, smirking. "She's Awira's sidekick, always defending her."

Nasrin's eyes narrowed. "And you're just Zoran's sidekick," she retorted sharply.

Asos's jaw dropped, caught off guard, as Nasrin swiveled and aimed the spray can at him. Her finger hovered over the nozzle, and she grinned mischievously. "Checkmate, bro."

She pressed the nozzle, and Asos flinched, hands raised in defence. "No!" he yelped, face scrunched in panic.

Only a faint hiss escaped the can – no paint, just air. Nasrin burst into laughter as Asos lowered his hands, his cheeks flushing red.

Even Zoran, usually too gruff for humour, let out a grudging chuckle. "A kid just owned you, Asos," he said, watching his friend's embarrassed silence.

* * *

Later that day, Arjan lined up with the other fighters for a grueling day of training. At the front, Commander Awira addressed the group with calm authority. "We've got to sharpen our aim. With threats growing daily, this is a skill we can't afford to neglect," she said, her voice both stern and motivating.

The fighters absorbed her words, bracing for the session ahead.

"Let's have Sahin lead today's bootcamp," Awira announced, gesturing toward the seasoned instructor. "She'll conduct a shooting drill that I expect all of you to learn from."

Sahin stepped forward, a taped-up rifle in hand, her confidence commanding immediate attention. "Load the magazine and pull back the operating rod," she instructed, demonstrating each step with practiced ease. Her eyes swept over the recruits, pausing briefly on Arjan. "Always check your firing direction before releasing the safety," she said, her tone steady but deliberate, the words landing with quiet emphasis.

Assuming a professional shooting stance, Sahin modeled the posture and grip needed for accurate shooting. Arjan watched intently, momentarily distracted by her poised demeanor and stern beauty.

Catching his lingering gaze, Sahin shot him a sharp look – a silent reprimand. Startled, Arjan quickly redirected his attention back to the intricacies of the drill.

"Place your finger on the trigger, buttstock against your shoulder, and grip the fore-stock with your off-hand," Sahin instructed. Taking aim at a moving target, she added, "Now, squeeze the trigger slowly," her focus unflinching.

The rifle cracked, the bullet striking the target square in the head. The fighters watched in silent admiration, awed by her precision.

"Bullseye! That's our headshot master in action. She's brilliant, isn't she?" Awira said, pride evident in her voice.

Applause rippled through the group, and Arjan felt a swell of pride as if Sahin was his protégé. From slaying knights on the battle screen to sniping jihadists on the battlefield, Sahin had blurred the line between virtual and reality.

Sahin gave a modest nod of acknowledgment to the applause before stepping aside and placing the rifle back in its crate.

"Thank you, Sahin," Awira said, stepping forward. "Now, let's have the freshers try. We could use a few more gunners around here."

Ron and Arjan exchanged a glance.

"Come on, give it a try," Awira urged, motioning for Ron to step up.

With a hesitant glance back at Arjan, Ron moved forward. At the sharp blast of Awira's whistle, he dashed to the weapon crate and grabbed a rifle. Halfway to the shooting line, his grip faltered, and the rifle thudded onto the dirt, drawing murmurs from the crowd.

Observing with a critical eye, Arjan was unimpressed. Such a mistake, he thought, was beneath him. A faint smirk tugged at his lips as he noted Ron's blunder.

"Relax, it happens. Try again," Awira reassured him.

His morale shaken, Ron trudged back to the start for another attempt.

While Arjan waited in the wings, he appeared undaunted. He'd watched Sahin translate her gaming skills to real combat. If gaming prowess was any indication, then he was more than ready. All these years of action games had to count for something, he thought to himself.

Another recruit stepped up to the drill, handling the rifle with apparent ease as he loaded the blank ammo and assumed a textbook stance. His smooth movements drew the attention of a few fighters, hinting at potential. But as he pulled the trigger, the rifle's recoil threw him off balance, and the shot went wide.

"Not bad. It's okay – everyone struggles at first," Sahin offered, her voice comforting as she tried to uplift the disheartened fighter.

"Not everyone," Arjan mused silently. In Arjan's defence, his confidence wasn't entirely misplaced. Video games, after all, are credited with sharpening reflexes and hand-eye coordination. Simulation games are widely used to hone the skills of pilots and surgeons, and even powerful militaries rely on them for recruitment, training, and strategy.

When Awira's whistle sounded, it was Arjan's turn. He sprinted to the ammunition crate, grabbing the rifle – but immediately flinched at its weight. It was far heavier than he'd expected, almost twenty times the familiar heft of a PlayStation controller. Struggling to adjust, he hauled the rifle to the shooting line, the weapon's bulk making it hard to find a steady stance.

Sahin watched from the sidelines, her expression unreadable.

Determined not to let her down, Arjan closed his eyes for a moment, took a deep breath, and hoisted the rifle onto his shoulder. Recalling every step from Sahin's demonstration, he reopened his eyes, locking on to the target with sharp focus.

"Go for it, Arjan! You can do it," Ron shouted, trying to buoy him up.

Arjan held his breath, aligning the sights. His trembling hands stilled as if by magic. His stance became rock solid, like a statue. Calmly, he squeezed the trigger, expecting the sharp report of the rifle. Instead, silence hung in the air – no gunshot, only the quiet click of a dry-fire. Confused, he glanced around, realizing something was amiss. His heart sank as the taunts began.

"Great shot, but guess who got killed?" Asos called mockingly.

"The newbie!" the group chanted in unison, erupting into laughter.

Arjan felt his face burn as he stood mortified.

"Enough!" Awira said sharply, silencing the jeers. "Arjan, you forgot to load the weapon," she explained, her tone blending reprimand with a touch of empathy.

"This isn't one of your video games, Noob!" Asos sneered, throwing in another barb.

"Asos, zip it. It's his first time. Go easy on him," Nasrin said firmly, her voice cutting through the continued ridicule as she stepped in to defend Arjan.

The insular bubble Arjan had been living in burst once again. He was tempted to shrug off the debacle as 'ludonarrative dissonance' – a gaming parlance for the mismatch between a game's narrative and its mechanics. But here, it felt more like the disconnect between reality and the imagined narrative in his head.

Sahin's expression remained unreadable, her poker face giving away nothing of her thoughts on the mishap.

With drooping shoulders and a face etched with embarrassment, Arjan returned to his spot. It was a sobering wake-up call – or perhaps it was a sign that he needed to carve out a different role for himself in this stark new reality.

14
Friendly Fire

Zoran was gearing up to lead his patrol team in a Toyota pickup truck when Commander Awira appeared, signaling them to stop.

"Hey! Wait up," her voice booming even over the sputtering engine.

Zoran turned off the ignition and hopped out. "Yes, Commander?" he asked.

"The brass wants the newcomers to start with something less challenging," Awira explained. "Help them ease into things."

"The foreigners?" Zoran asked with a hint of disbelief.

Awira arched an eyebrow. "What foreigners? They're one of us now."

"Fine, but I don't have time to babysit," Zoran grumbled as he glanced back at the truck, itching to get going.

"It's not a request, Zoran," Awira said firmly, ending the discussion. She scanned the area and barked, "Arjan, Ron, on your feet!"

The two scrambled up at her command, exchanging bewildered glances.

"You're on patrol duty, effective immediately. Move out!" Awira ordered, her tone brooking no hesitation.

With a resigned sigh, Zoran led the group along the patrol route. Arjan and Ron, wide-eyed and uncertain, followed as the patrol wound through a war-torn landscape. Buildings lay in crumbling ruins, and the streets stood eerily abandoned.

Arjan, struck by the devastation, couldn't tear his eyes away. Feeling a deep pull to document what he was witnessing, he grabbed a camcorder from the truck. He pressed record, and words poured from him, his impromptu commentary filling the silence around them. "Innocents have been murdered, and entire city blocks reduced to rubble in this senseless war. What was once a bustling city is now a ghost town," he narrated, his voice heavy with emotion as the camera swept across the ruins of Kobani.

Zoran and Asos exchanged grimaces at Arjan's commentary. Though earnest, his words felt naive and simplistic. To the seasoned fighters, Arjan's eagerness to document every detail made him come across as tone-deaf, as if he were making light of the suffering they had endured. To some, his act seemed to reduce their painful reality to a spectacle – a superficial take on a situation far more complex and nuanced than his lens could ever capture.

Holding the camera steady, Arjan continued, his tone becoming more urgent. "It's not just about the Kurds; the whole of humanity faces the threat of ISIS."

Observing the growing annoyance among the team, Nasrin nudged him discreetly. "That camera is only meant for reconnaissance... put it away," she whispered.

Startled, Arjan muttered, "Sorry," his voice faltering as he quickly stowed the camera, his earlier fervour dampened by the weight of his mistake.

Nasrin offered him a small, understanding smile and a nod toward the group, a silent reminder to be mindful of the group's dynamics and the sensitivity of their mission.

Moments later, the patrol hit a rubble-strewn street. The fighters dismounted and continued on foot, navigating a landscape of utter devastation – collapsed buildings, shattered lives spilling onto the streets.

As they waded through the ravages, Arjan's gaze fell on a toy gun smeared with dried blood, wedged among broken stones and twisted metal. The sight hit him like a punch in the gut, stopping him dead in his tracks while the others moved ahead. Compelled by a mix of horror and curiosity, Arjan drifted away from the safety of his group to get a closer look.

As Arjan reached down to pick up the knock-off Nerf gun, his fingers barely brushed the plastic when Asos spun around, alarm flashing in his eyes. "What the hell are you doing? That could be a booby trap! Don't!" he shouted, his voice echoing through the desolate street.

The fighters instantly tightened their formation, weapons raised, scanning their surroundings for danger.

Arjan froze, the toy gun in hand, now the centre of intense, wary stares. Slowly, he raised his hands in surrender, the toy dangling awkwardly from his grip.

"Drop that fucking thing right now! Now!" Zoran bellowed, the raw edge in his voice betraying fear for his team's safety.

"Relax, it's just a toy," Nasrin intervened, her voice calm yet firm. She stepped toward Arjan, lowering her voice. "Don't do that again, Arjan. It could have been a bomb."

Zoran's frustration had been simmering for days, fuelled by Arjan's missteps. This time, it boiled over. "What do you think you are? A fucking hero?" he spat, anger breaking free.

Arjan recoiled, the weight of Zoran's words hitting him harder than the reality around them.

"It's okay, Zoran. He gets it now," Nasrin said, trying to defuse the tension.

"Nasrin, stop defending his stupid antics! He's going to get all of us killed," Zoran snapped, his patience frayed to the limit. Turning away, he muttered under his breath, still simmering with anger.

Nasrin sighed and turned to Arjan, her voice softer. "Please, let it go."

Arjan nodded, pale and silent, as he carefully set the toy gun back on the ground. He stepped away, treating it as if it might still betray him. Despite his shame, he glanced at Nasrin, his eyes conveying deep gratitude for her support.

The group resumed their patrol, shaking their heads in quiet disapproval. Arjan lingered a step behind, tears stinging his eyes. He felt more alienated than ever, caught between his desire to contribute and the reality of his mistakes. Trudging forward, he grappled with a growing sense of inadequacy, unsure of his place within the team.

* * *

As the truck rattled through the ghostly streets, its echoes a hollow reminder of the day's tensions, Arjan sat slumped in the back. His face pale as ash, stared blankly at the ruins outside. His eyes, normally sharp with curiosity, were glazed over with exhaustion. Beside him, Ron attempted small talk, but his words were swallowed by the steady hum of the engine.

Back at the base, the team gathered around a makeshift dining table cobbled together from scavenged wood. The room buzzed with the clatter of plates and low murmurs of conversation. In stark contrast, Arjan sat motionless, his plate untouched, his fork idle in his hand.

His mind churned, replaying the day's events in an endless loop. Ron, seated beside him, threw occasional worried glances but chose to respect the silence. Arjan, usually brimming with energy and eagerness to prove himself, now seemed hollow, a shadow of his former self.

Sahin noticed the change from the table across from her. Concern tugged at her features as she glanced at Nasrin beside her. "What's going on with Arjan?" she asked, her voice low, barely audible over the din of the dining hall, but laced with worry.

Nasrin sighed, following Sahin's gaze to the sombre figure. "Zoran," she replied simply, the name heavy with unspoken meaning. She shifted in her seat, as if searching for the right words. "He lost it on Arjan during the patrol – over a toy gun he picked up on the street."

Sahin's expression darkened. "Again? That's the second time this week. This can't just be about a toy gun."

"It's more than that," Nasrin admitted, her voice a whisper almost stifled by the surrounding chatter. "Arjan's trying hard, but he keeps getting into these situations. And Zoran… well, he doesn't think Arjan's cut out for this. It's taking a toll."

Sahin's gaze never left Arjan, watching him as if trying to read the thoughts swirling in his head. "What do you think?" she asked.

Nasrin hesitated, her eyes thoughtful. "He's young and inexperienced, but he has potential. What he needs is guidance, not condemnation. And he has the drive to learn and do better."

Sahin nodded, her mind made up as she stood. "I'll talk to Zoran. Discipline is one thing, but breaking someone's spirit is another." She paused, glancing at Nasrin. "Do you think Zoran knows Arjan came here because of me?"

Nasrin hesitated before replying, "Of course. His sidekicks saw you two." She met Sahin's gaze briefly, then added, "Maybe that's why he's so hard on Arjan. He won't let him slack at all."

Sahin stood still, shaking her head. The weight of the situation settled over her, leaving her unsure of what to say.

* * *

As the midday sun cast stark shadows across the base, most fighters sought refuge in the communal area for lunch.

From the war room, Commander Awira's voice rang out, crisp and urgent, "Sahin! Zoran! Report to the war room, now."

Stationed at the gate, Zoran gave a brisk nod before scanning the vicinity for his second-in-command. His searching gaze landed on Arjan, sitting alone on the verandah, seemingly lost in thought. "Hey! Where's Asos?" Zoran barked.

Startled, Arjan looked up, momentarily confused. He pointed to himself. "Me? Are you talking to me?" Given that Zoran typically saw through him, Arjan's skepticism was reasonable.

"Don't waste my time. Have you seen Asos?" Zoran snapped, impatience edging his tone.

"I don't know," Arjan replied hesitantly, studying Zoran's demeanor. After a pause, he ventured, "Can I help you?"

Zoran froze briefly, his sharp eyes reassessing Arjan. "Of course, you can help me. Get over here."

Arjan was caught off guard. He had offered to help out of courtesy, never expecting Zoran to take him up on it. Rising to his feet, he hesitantly approached.

"I want you to be our lookout while I'm in the meeting," Zoran said, his voice laced with reluctant trust.

"Really? What am I supposed to do?" Arjan asked, eyebrows furrowed.

Zoran unslung his binoculars and placed them around Arjan's neck. "Keep an eye out and alert us at the first sign of movement," he instructed firmly.

"Got it," Arjan replied, straightening, his voice steady with a newfound sense of purpose. "Keep your head on a swivel. I don't want any blunders here," Zoran warned before walking off.

Arjan hunkered down behind the sandbag nest, his senses watchful at first but dulling with every passing minute. The task wasn't half as exciting as he had imagined. Time dragged as the silent, unchanging landscape stretched before him. Minutes passed without movement or anything remotely interesting. Arjan's attention kept drifting to Sahin's sniper rifle, which was left unattended on the range. At first, he resisted the temptation, but it became impossible to ignore. The rifle gleamed in the sun, almost daring him, a reminder of the skill he was itching to prove. Just one shot couldn't hurt, he reasoned. After all, being taken off combat training for one bad miss didn't exactly seem fair. With the area seemingly clear, he set the binoculars down and walked to the range, leaving his post unguarded.

He mounted the formidable Zagros rifle on its bipod, loaded it as he'd been taught, and took a deep breath. Carefully, he lined up his sights on an empty spray can near the graffiti wall, ready to demonstrate his skill. Adjusting the gauge, he slowly squeezed the trigger. The recoil jolted him as the shot missed, striking a sandbag instead.

Meanwhile, in the mud-brick war room, tension filled the air.

"We have grave news from the eastern front," Awira said, her tone heavy. "The SFA has been overrun by Daesh. They fought valiantly, but Al-Nusra Front reinforced Daesh at a critical moment."

"What? That can't be true. Daesh and Al-Qaida are sworn enemies," Zoran interjected.

"Not anymore. They've brokered some sort of truce to defeat us," Sahin said grimly.

"This proves they're indeed colluding against us," Awira confirmed.

The alliance between Al-Nusra Front and ISIS, two of the most lethal militant groups, was a devastating blow to the Kurds' already slim chances of survival. With Kobani's southern and eastern fronts captured, ISIS was swiftly tightening its grip on the base.

"Shouldn't we rush to help the SFA? There's going to be a massacre," Sahin urged.

"It's too late. They've lost the radio tower. Without communication, sending reinforcements would be walking into a trap," Awira said flatly.

"So, we just let them die?" Sahin pressed, frustration edging into her voice.

"We can't let emotions guide us," Awira said firmly. "I've instructed the surviving commanders to fall back and regroup with us."

"Awira's right," Zoran said. "It could be a trap to scatter our forces, leaving our base vulnerable. Ultimately, that's what they are after. We must remain cautious."

"For now, we monitor the situation. I hope the SFA fighters can make it to us," Awira said. Her words, however, did little to abate Sahin's dissatisfaction.

Back at the range, Arjan took another shot. CLANK! The bullet missed again, ricocheting off the wrought-iron entry gate.

On the other side, Jamie and a few Kurdish civilians ducked, flailing in alarm at the unexpected gunfire. Raising both arms, Jamie shouted, "We're friendlies! Don't shoot! Don't shoot!"

Recognizing the voice, Arjan lowered the rifle, squinting toward the gate. His heart skipped a beat as he spotted Jamie. Dropping the rifle, he rushed over. "Jamie? Jamie!"

"God, you're alive?" he exclaimed, disbelief and joy thick in his voice.

Unlatching the gate, he pulled Jamie into a tight embrace. Jamie, equally stunned, stammered, "Oh my god, Arjan… It's you! How did you get here?"

"Holy fuck! I can't believe this," Arjan said, turning toward the camp. "Ron! Look who's here!"

Ron emerged from his tent, gawked in shock, then broke into a grin. He sprinted over and joined the embrace.

"How did you guys make it out alive?" Jamie asked with genuine curiosity.

"It's a long story," Ron replied. "What about you? We thought you were gone after we heard those gunshots."

Jamie's face clouded briefly. "That must've been our poor driver. I was lucky enough to escape," he said, his casual tone at odds with the haunted look in his eyes.

"All this time, I wished I could help you guys, but I didn't know where they'd taken you. I'm so sorry," Jamie said, his tone guilt-ridden.

"C'mon! Don't say that," Arjan said, clapping him on the shoulder. "Look, we're still alive. And now we're reunited!"

"Thank God for that!" Jamie's gaze wandered over the camp before returning to his friends. "Where's Ahmed?"

Arjan and Ron exchanged a sombre glance. "He wasn't as lucky as us," Ron said quietly.

Jamie's face fell. "God bless his soul," he murmured as they shared a brief moment of silence for their fallen comrade.

Breaking the sombre mood, Arjan asked, "How did you find us?"

"Ever since the SFA saved me, I've been fighting alongside them," Jamie began, his tone heavy. "Yesterday, Daesh and Al-Qaida attacked our eastern front. The bloody jihadists have taken the industrial zone. Your commander asked us to pull back and regroup here." He glanced at the civilians behind him, his voice faltering. "I could only save these few."

Arjan and Ron looked at the displaced group with compassion.

"Some of our fighters are still trying to rescue more. I hope they make it," Jamie added.

"You're a hero, Jamie," Ron said, patting him on the back.

Jamie nodded modestly, but Arjan noticed his wounded arm. "You're hurt! Come on, let's get that treated," he said, ushering Jamie and the six civilians – a mix of men, women, and an infant in tattered ethnic garments – into the safety of the base.

"Ron, get Nasrin to arrange for them. I'll stay on guard," Arjan instructed, his tone urgent.

Ron nodded and, as he helped Jamie to the infirmary, struck up a conversation, eager to hear more about his harrowing journey.

* * *

As dusk settled over the base, the dining area buzzed with casual chatter, the air rich with the aroma of spices. The floor was strewn with a large plastic tablecloth, where Arjan, Ron, Jamie, and other fighters sat cross-legged, surrounding a spread of traditional Kurdish cuisine. The spread included *dolma* – rice-and-meat-stuffed vegetables, thin flatbreads, and a shared bowl of tangy *mastaw*. A small portion of dried plums and strawberries, wrinkled with age, lent a quiet sweetness to the savoury fare.

"We are so happy to have you back," Arjan said, passing a plate of dolma to Jamie.

"Really? That explains your welcoming me with a freaking gunfire salute. You nearly killed me back there," Jamie said with a chuckle, though the humour couldn't fully mask the hint of concern in his voice.

"I was just trying out the sniper. I'm such a bot," Arjan admitted, scooping up a stuffed pepper with a grin, trying to downplay the mishap.

"He was probably testing whether friendly fire works in the real world," Ron quipped, earning laughter from the group.

Jamie's expression shifted as a thought struck him. He nudged Arjan. "Hey, how are your parents? Did Indian intelligence visit them?"

Arjan's smile faded, his eyebrows shooting up in alarm. He glanced around nervously, hoping no one had overheard. Jamie immediately realized his mistake.

"Oh, sorry! My bad," Jamie murmured, regret colouring his tone.

Leaning closer, Arjan whispered, "I've already caused them enough grief. I hope intelligence doesn't trouble them now."

"Have you checked on them recently?" Jamie asked.

"There's no way to. I lost my phone. I have not contacted them since," Arjan replied, frustration creeping into his voice.

"You can use mine," Jamie offered, pulling out his mobile.

Arjan shook his head. "There's no service here."

Jamie frowned, checking his phone. "Oh, right. No signal."

"We're totally disconnected from the outside world," Ron lamented.

"Maybe you could hack into one of the Turkish networks across the border," Jamie thought aloud.

Arjan considered it, nodding slowly. "That's actually a good idea."

Jamie smirked. "The Turks won't let our Peshmerga fighters through. The least they could do is offer us free internet."

"You've got a hack for everything, don't you?" Arjan said with a grin.

"I'm not sure it'll work, but it's worth a shot," Jamie replied.

As the evening progressed, Nasrin stood up, clearing her throat to capture everyone's attention for some stand-up comedy. "What did the suicide bomber tell his jihadi students?" She paused for effect, then grinned. "Pay attention. I'm only going to do this once."

The room erupted in laughter as Jamie rolled his eyes, glancing back at Arjan and Ron.

Raising a hand to quiet the crowd, Nasrin launched into another one. "An ISIS member stopped a Christian couple at a checkpoint and asked, 'Are you Muslim?' The husband replied, 'Yes.' The thug demanded a *Quran* verse. The man calmly recited a random *Bible* verse, and the ISIS member let them go. Furious, the wife later asked why he took such a risk. The man replied, 'If they'd actually read the *Quran*, they wouldn't be killing people.'"

Laughter and applause filled the room, even earning a nod of approval from Commander Awira. "Good one, Nasrin. That was deep," Awira said.

Arjan couldn't help but feel a surge of admiration for Nasrin and the other young girls in the faction who had taken up arms at such a tender age. It was an age of studying, putting up makeup and gossiping with friends. They weren't even old enough to play violent video games, for God's sake. But here they were warring against the world's most lethal terror outfit. Yet, they smiled, laughed, and stood firm in the face of death.

"Who's next?" Nasrin asked, scanning the room for volunteers.

Ron's hand shot up. "I've got one!" he exclaimed eagerly.

Arjan and Jamie turned, their surprise evident as Nasrin gestured for Ron to come forward. Grinning, Ron leapt to his feet and approached what passed for a stage.

"It better be good," Arjan muttered to Jamie, sinking lower to the floor in anticipation of secondhand embarrassment.

"What do you call ISIS when it's dead?" Ron posed the question as the fighters exchanged puzzled looks. "WAS-WAS!" he delivered, grinning at his punchline.

A few chuckles rippled through the crowd, though Arjan and Jamie cringed, exchanging mortified looks before covering their faces with their hands.

"If we ever run out of ammo, we could just broadcast his jokes over the megaphone to scare off the enemy," Arjan quipped, shaking his head.

"Seriously! I'm already starting to miss the sound of gunfire," Jamie said, his laughter tinged with irony.

Arjan widened his eyes in mock horror. "Damn! That was dark," he replied, unable to suppress a grin.

Amidst the muffled laughter drifting from the dining area, Zoran stayed outside, using the quiet of the evening to focus on his physical training. Under the dim entrance lights, he was absorbed in a makeshift weightlifting session, bench-pressing a barbell rigged with sandbags instead of conventional weights. Each fierce grunt echoed as he pushed upward, his focus unshaken – until Asos's hurried footsteps broke his rhythm.

"Comrade Zoran! I need to talk to you," Asos called out, urgency in his tone.

"Can't you see I'm in the middle of a sesh?" Zoran snapped, irritation flashing across his face.

"It's important. It's about Arjan," Asos insisted, catching his breath.

"What's lover boy done now?" Zoran asked mid-lift, sarcasm threading his tone, expecting some trivial misadventure.

Asos leaned closer, his voice lowering. "Eylo overheard him talking to his friends. He's apparently wanted by Indian intelligence."

"What?" The word burst from Zoran as he abruptly let the barbell crash down with a heavy thud.

"That's what Eylo claims. He sounded pretty certain," Asos added, aware that he had Zoran's full attention.

Wiping sweat from his brow, Zoran sat up on the wooden bench, his expression turning grave.

"Could he be an ISIS spy? What do we do?" Asos's accusation hung heavy in the air.

Zoran rose to his full height, his presence commanding as he squared up to Asos. Dusting off his palms, his features were set with cold fury. "If this is true, I'll choke that traitor with my bare hands," he growled, his voice dripping with menace.

Suddenly the jovial atmosphere inside the base seemed a world away, contrasting sharply with the weight of war and the creeping shadows of suspicion now threatening to fracture their ranks.

15
Taste of Blood

On a cold night in Kobani, silence enveloped the base, broken only by the soft whispers of wind and the occasional shuffle of sentinels. Most fighters were deep in sleep, seeking respite from the day's hardships.

Inside his tent, however, Arjan lay restless. Tossing and turning in his cot, he struggled with stubborn congestion that made every breath a battle. Shifting uncomfortably, he recalled Jamie mentioning a homemade concoction his grandmother swore by for clearing sinuses.

Spurred by the prospect of relief, Arjan pushed the heavy blanket aside and swung his legs off the cot. Slipping into his boots, he grabbed his jacket and stepped into the crisp night air, intent on finding Jamie and the magical recipe. Approaching Jamie's tent, he found it empty, the sleeping bag folded and untouched. "Where could he be?" Arjan muttered, scratching his head. Deciding to check back later, he turned away.

With time to spare, Arjan wandered into the control room. Spotting a camcorder beside the computer, he felt a sudden impulse. Sitting down, he connected the device and began transferring recent patrol footage from Kobani. Once the footage was secured, he turned to the next challenge: finding an internet connection.

His fingers flew across the keyboard as he broke into a nearby Turkish network. "God bless Jamie," he said with a faint smile when he finally gained backdoor access. Wondering why he hadn't thought of this sooner, Arjan quickly composed a heartfelt message to his parents, pouring out his emotions to reassure them of his safety. With a deep breath, he hit send and began uploading his videos.

As the upload bar crept across the screen, the faint sound of light and floppy footsteps suddenly pierced the quiet. Arjan tensed, his attention snapping to the sound. The steps seemed cautious, almost secretive. His curiosity piqued, Arjan rose and followed the noise.

Rounding a corner, he stopped cold at an unusual sight: the flap of Sahin's tent hung ajar. Moving cautiously, he peered inside. The dim light revealed a startling scene: Jamie stood beside Awira and Sahin's cots, murmuring a verse, eyes tightly shut. Arjan's heart raced as Jamie reached into his jacket, his hand hovering as if for a trigger.

"Jamie!" Arjan's voice tore through the silence, a desperate attempt to disrupt whatever was about to unfold.

Jamie was staggered. Sahin and Awira, abruptly roused from sleep, stared in disbelief.

"Hands up, Jamie!" Arjan demanded, his voice steady despite the turmoil.

"I'm going to blow these women up," Jamie spat, nodding toward Sahin with disdain. "Especially this hellcat bitch."

Arjan tensed, ready to spring forward, but Jamie's next words froze him. "Don't try anything stupid. My finger's on the trigger. Nothing can save you now."

Reluctantly, Arjan raised his hands in submission, while Awira and Sahin looked on helplessly.

"Why are you doing this, Jamie? You're one of us," Arjan pleaded, trying to reach the man he thought he knew.

"I never belonged here," Jamie said coldly. "I came here to kill this infidel."

"Stop this madness, I'm begging you," Arjan beseeched, his voice breaking.

Sahin and Awira began to rise slowly, tension visible in their movements.

"She and her fighters denied our martyrs their glory. She deserves to die," Jamie declared. As he reached into his jacket, Sahin lunged for a gun beside her cot, but Jamie was quicker – he kicked out at her, sending her stumbling back.

"No, no, no! Don't make this harder!" Jamie cautioned.

Distracted, Jamie didn't notice Arjan creeping toward the tent entrance. Snatching up an assault rifle, Arjan aimed it unsteadily at him.

"Careful, kid! That's not a toy," Jamie taunted, unshaken by the barrel pointed at him.

Arjan's palms were clammy; his aim wavered even at close range.

"Who are you kidding? I dare you to shoot me… c'mon," Jamie jeered, his laughter echoing mockingly in the tense air.

The commotion had drawn fighters outside the tent, now watching the standoff in shock. Despite his trembling hands, Arjan kept the rifle trained on Jamie.

"Okay then. Let's see who pulls the trigger first. Seems fun, eh?" Jamie challenged, reaching deeper into his jacket.

Arjan swallowed a lump in his throat, fear and resolve mingling in his eyes.

"On my count," Jamie started, a cruel smirk on his face.

"Please... don't make me do this," Arjan stammered, his hands shaking visibly.

"Three," Jamie counted aloud.

The fighters outside stirred as panicked murmurs erupted - jagged, overlapping, charged with dread.

"Two," Jamie continued.

Before Jamie could count down to one, Arjan's instincts – sharpened not by combat but by countless hours on video game controllers – took over. He reflexively pre-fired. The gunshot was thunderous. Jamie's head recoiled violently as the bullet struck, sending a horrific spray of blood across the tent. Stunned by his own actions, Arjan stood frozen, the grim reality of the moment sinking in.

Sahin and Awira quickly overcame their initial paralysis and sprang into action. They rushed to Jamie's body and tore off his jacket, revealing the suicide belt strapped to his chest. They scrambled to disarm the explosives.

Outside, cheers and war cries erupted. The fighters gathered around Arjan, patting his back in grim recognition of his life-saving act. Arjan walked out, dazed and blood-spattered, his ears still ringing from the gunshot.

In the midst of the tumult, Zoran burst through the crowd, his face contorted with rage. He seized Arjan by the collar and slammed him against the wall. The cheers turned to gasps as the fighters stared, astonished by the turn of events.

"You're not a fucking hero! You are a traitor. You brought this danger upon us!" Zoran bellowed.

"What… what are you talking about?" Arjan croaked, barely able to speak under Zoran's furious glare.

"Jamie was your friend. You let him into the base," Zoran accused.

Sahin intervened, rushing to Arjan's defence. "Zoran, stop this! Let him go," she pleaded.

"Ah, here comes the ladylove," Zoran sneered, turning his scorn on Sahin

"He's not a traitor. I've known him for a long time," Sahin asserted.

"Oh really? From the internet? How reliable," Zoran retorted. "Did you know he's wanted by his own country's intelligence?"

"What?" the word escaped Sahin in disbelief.

"He fled his country to join ISIS," Zoran declared.

The accusation sent shockwaves through the crowd. Fighters raised their weapons, the ominous click of safeties disengaging resonated through the air.

"That's not true, Sahin. I can explain… listen to me," Arjan stammered, his plea intensifying as he felt the deadly threat escalate around him.

"Save your explanations for your God," Zoran snarled, his grip tightening around Arjan's collar. Arjan struggled futilely against the iron hold, completely overpowered by Zoran's brute force.

"Stop it, Zoran! I trust him with my life. He cannot be a traitor. Let him go!" Sahin cried out, her voice quivering with desperation.

Her appeals went unheeded as Zoran began to strangle Arjan. Sahin's cries grew shriller. Arjan's face reddened as he struggled to breathe under the crushing hold.

"Zoran! Stand down!" Awira's voice cut through the chaos. "He just saved all our lives."

"No, he killed his friend to cover his tracks! He's saving his own skin," Zoran argued bitterly, his grip unwavering.

"It is an order, Zoran!" Awira commanded sharply.

With a clenched jaw, Zoran released his grip. Arjan collapsed to his knees, coughing and gasping for air. Zoran turned to Sahin, his glare venomous. "Defending a traitor makes you one too. Next time, he won't be so lucky." With that chilling warning, he stormed off, leaving a heavy silence in his wake.

As the tension slowly dissipated, the fighters began to disperse, murmuring among themselves. A few stayed behind, helping Arjan to his feet as he struggled to regain his breath.

* * *

The next morning, Arjan sat alone on the verandah, grappling with the aftermath of a harrowing night. The sequence had unfolded like a nightmarish rollercoaster, leaving his psyche in tatters. He had gone from foiling an assassination plot and taking the life of someone he once called a friend, to being branded a spy and nearly losing his own life in the ensuing chaos. He hadn't even begun to find his bearings in this unforgiving world when a tidal wave of accusations swept him further into the margins. From comrade to pariah in mere moments, he now felt like a persona non grata among those he had come to help.

The glances from the other fighters, filled with suspicion and contempt, burned into him, deepening the divide between him and the unit. He felt lost, alone, and unsure of his place. Watching Arjan slumped in desolation, Sahin's heart went out to him. It pained her to see him so burdened, especially knowing he had endured these trials for her sake. She set her weapon on a crate and approached him. Pulling up a chair, she sat down beside him.

"How are you holding up?" she inquired gently.

Her voice broke through Arjan's reverie. "I'm okay," he replied, though his voice betrayed the strain he was under.

"I'm sorry for what Zoran did," she said after a pause. "We live under constant threat here. It's hard not to feel insecure."

"Don't defend him," Arjan cut in sharply. "He's had a personal vendetta against me ever since I set foot here. He's been out to get me since day one. I came all this way to help, and they are accusing me of being a fucking spy. They're baying for my blood," he added bitterly.

She listened quietly, letting him vent.

"They even ransacked my tent, trying to pin something on me. So much for gratitude," he scoffed, shaking his head.

After a pause, she asked quietly, "Really? You came all this way to help them?"

Caught off guard, Arjan hesitated, unsure how to respond.

"None of this would've happened if you'd just eloped with me. But no, you had to stay, leaving me no choice," he lamented, shifting blame.

"Are you seriously blaming me now?" Sahin shot back. "I warned you. I told you to walk away."

Arjan wrung his hands in frustration. "I'm sorry. I'm on edge. I can't come to grips with the fact that I killed someone – let alone someone I thought was a friend."

"You did the right thing. Jamie was an ISIS spy," she reassured him.

"But I'm not a spy, Sahin. I came here only for you. You trust me, don't you?" he pressed, searching her eyes for affirmation.

"I'm insulted you'd even ask," she replied, her voice softening. "Of course I trust you. I know you're not a spy. As for the others, we're working to convince them of your innocence. My entire unit saw you and Ron nearly executed by ISIS."

Arjan puckered an eyebrow, sarcasm dripping from his voice. "Thank God for ISIS, or I'd have no evidence to prove my innocence."

"That's not true. I would always stand by you. You know that, right?" she replied earnestly, her sincerity cutting through his cynicism.

"I'm sorry. It just feels like the whole world is against me. Everywhere I turn, I see enemies. Nothing I do is right. I'm trying to prove myself but I keep failing miserably," he muttered.

"It's okay," she said with a tired smile. "Remember what they say – if video games have taught us anything, it's that encountering enemies means you're headed in the right direction."

"But they never mentioned that even your allies would turn out to be enemies," he said, the irony not lost on him as he reflected on the bitter twist.

Sahin hesitated, momentarily at a loss. Arjan, overwhelmed, crouched forward, burying his head in his hands.

Seeking to lighten the mood, Sahin changed the subject. "Speaking of video games, how are Faiz, Eitan, and Zafar? How are they doing?" she asked, her tone brightening.

"They are fine," Arjan said, his voice softening with nostalgia. "Ah, the good old days… life was so carefree. Who would've thought our lives would take such a drastic turn. I was waiting so eagerly to see you in Munich."

Sahin nodded with a sigh. "By the way, what happened to the championship?"

"Guess who won it?" he said, a small smile creeping in, "None other than our very own Squad Aces!"

"Are you serious?" her eyes widened in surprise.

"Yes," he replied, his smile broadening.

"Oh my God! That is so cool," she exclaimed.

"Yeah, but it was bittersweet. We thought you were dead, so it was pretty sombre the whole time. We even dedicated the trophy to you," he said, pausing with a wry smile, "Again, because we thought you were dead."

"Wow! I'm touched by the tribute. Although it's kind of weird since you know, I am not dead yet," Sahin replied, playing along to keep the mood light.

Arjan chuckled, shaking his head. "We disbanded our squad after the tournament."

"Really?"

"Faiz, Zafar, and Eitan formed a hacktivist group called Anonym-Aces," he revealed.

"Seriously? I've heard of them. They disrupted Daesh's online operations for weeks."

"That was them. But I guess those attacks must've been nothing more than minor inconveniences to ISIS. It's not like we were fighting on the ground," he said.

"That's not true. ISIS relies heavily on online recruitment. If anything, I believe cyber-attacks might just be a secret weapon to bring them to their knees," she reckoned, her voice trailing off as she fell into contemplative silence.

Noticing the catch in her voice, Arjan turned to face her. "Hey, what's wrong?" he asked gently.

Sahin quickly wiped her eyes, brushing away tears. "Nothing," she murmured, her voice thick with emotion. "I'm just touched by how everyone has come together to support me. I really appreciate it."

"Hey! Don't forget – I'm the one who came all the way to Syria for you."

Arjan's wisecrack drew an abrupt chuckle from Sahin. As their laughter faded, a quiet moment settled between them. Their eyes met, and in that unspoken beat, the spark of their once-lost love flickered anew.

Their reverie was interrupted by Nasrin's urgent approach, "Arjan! Did you post a video online?"

"Yeah. Now what wrong did I do?" Arjan said, throwing his hands up in surrender.

"Arjan, the vlog you uploaded – it's gone viral," Nasrin said, breathless.

"What?" Sahin gasped, while Arjan rolled his eyes in disbelief, muttering, "You've got to be kidding me."

* * *

While Arjan was losing favour at the Kurdish base – a silent transformation was unfolding. Unbeknownst to him, his YouTube videos were skyrocketing in popularity, resonating far beyond the war-torn confines of his camp. The more his voice was drowned out by a chorus of baseless allegations, the louder it echoed across the globe. While his comrades cast him aside, strangers from distant lands were rising in his defence. Unaware of the burgeoning support and heartfelt messages pouring into his channel, he faced abandonment in his immediate world even as a global embrace awaited him.

Within twenty-four hours, his vlog soared to YouTube's trending charts. The explosive spread of his story caught the eye of major news outlets, captivated not only by the harrowing visuals but also by the poignant narrative at its heart – an ordinary man's daring journey to rescue his love from the clutches of ISIS. As hashtags like #LoveOverISIS and #KobaniHero flourished across social media, the world tuned in. His raw footage of Kobani's devastation was unlike anything the public had seen, evoking both intrigue and empathy. Among the millions watching were his parents, moved to tears by the dire circumstances their son faced.

The video's impact went beyond virality. It sparked renewed international focus on Kobani. Arjan's sharp criticism of Turkey's inaction and the looming ISIS threat forced global organizations to act.

Stirred by the outcry, the United Nations pressured Turkish authorities to open borders for aid and reinforcements. Emergency treaties were drafted to facilitate the flow of volunteers and military supplies into the besieged city.

Back at the base, emotions ran high. While the global attention offered a glimmer of hope, it also magnified the immense gravity of their situation. Fighters clustered around the flickering screen of an old CRT television in the mess hall, watching their plight broadcast across news channels. Arjan was lauded for his efforts, which had shone a light on their struggle. Sahin applauded with pride, blinking back tears, while many fighters expressed both gratitude and remorse for having doubted him. Zoran, however, remained skeptical.

Despite these developments, the situation remained precarious. The Kurdish resistance was gaining momentum, but tangible aid was slow to arrive. As Kurdish fighters battled ISIS, world leaders and the UN warned of an impending bloodbath. Diplomatic efforts intensified, yet Turkish forces stood frustratingly idle, just a stone's throw from the battleground, despite escalating calls for intervention. The hope sparked by Arjan's efforts was real, but uncertainty continued to cast its shadow.

* * *

The new day brought with it a hint of redemption for Arjan. After his recent exploits, the faction's stance toward him softened. Not only was he welcomed back, but he was also reinstated to weapon training – a nod that felt much like a promotion within their ranks.

On the training field, as Arjan adjusted his posture and refined his trigger pull, he noticed glances of approval from other fighters. His reputation, once marred by suspicion, was beginning to mend, inch by inch.

Amidst the rattle of gunfire and sharp tang of gunpowder, Sahin's arrival at the edge of the field interrupted his focus. Her delicate features, offset by the harshness of battle fatigues and a slung sniper rifle, made her a captivating paradox – a seamless blend of beauty and beast. Yet, it was her smile, gentle and disarming, that always caught Arjan off guard.

"Arjan! Can I talk to you?" Sahin asked.

Dusting himself off, Arjan quickly caught up with her, falling in step along the boundary wall.

Sahin's expression hardened. "Daesh has taken Tel Shair Hill on the western front. We're surrounded – they can shell us from the east, south, and west," she said, her voice steady despite the grim news.

"They're cutting off every escape route. This might be your last chance to leave," she added, her gaze scanning the horizon for danger.

As Arjan was about to respond, she raised a hand, stopping him mid-thought. "No rash decisions. I need you to be sure about this. Once they close in, there will be no way out. Please think about it carefully," she cautioned.

He paused, not to collect his thoughts but because she asked him to. Then he said what he was going to say anyway, "Do you really think I'll leave you behind and go? Sahin, tell me. Have I come all the way only to abandon you?"

"Arjan! You've done enough. Please get back to safety while you can. Think about your parents," she implored.

Arjan's reply was filled with unwavering hope. "I believe the world will wake up to our plight. I'm sure they will intervene."

"ISIS isn't going to wait for that. They have already stepped up their onslaught… There is no time," she countered, her tone urgent.

"My decision is final, Sahin. We stand together in this fight, and we'll see it through together," he declared.

Sahin fell silent, her arguments exhausted. She lowered her gaze, her voice soft. "As much as it comforts me to have you here, I'm terrified of losing you. I've already lost too much. I can't bear to lose you too."

Arjan stepped closer, gently placing his finger on her lips. "Shhh, no more. I'm staying. End of discussion."

Sahin sighed, a hint of exasperation in her voice. "Why are you so stubborn?"

"I'm not stubborn, Sahin. I just want to stand by you, no matter what," he replied with a faint smile.

She sighed, resigned but touched. "Okay. I give up. But promise me, you'll stay close during gunfights. I'll watch over you."

"Just like you did in video games?" Arjan asked teasingly, knowing full well how much it would trigger her.

Sahin shook her head, unable to suppress a smile. "Yes, Arjan! Just like in video games."

Their smiles lingered until Arjan's voice wavered, overwhelmed by the rush of emotions. "I love you, Sahin. Do you love me?"

Her reply was soft but steady. "I do, Arjan. But maybe we'll have to save our love story for another life."

"Another life? But YOLO," Arjan quipped, his tone light.

Sahin frowned, puzzled. "YOLO?"

"You only live once," he explained, shaking his head. "Don't you remember SRK's dialogue?" Arjan launched into a perfect imitation of Shahrukh Khan's iconic line, *"Hum ek baar jeete hai, ek baar marte hai, shaadi bhi ek baar hoti hai, aur pyaar bhi…"* (We live once, we die once, we marry once, and we fall in love…)

Sahin's lips curved into a smile as she finished it for him, *"…ek hi baar hota hai."* (…happens only once.)

"See? SRK was onto YOLO way before it was cool," Arjan joked.

Their hands intertwined as they exchanged a long, heartfelt gaze. In that moment, despite the chaos and uncertainty closing in around them, they found solace in each other's commitment. They embraced tightly, drawing strength from the shared resolve that bound them together.

16
End Game

As the first light of dawn streaked across the sky above Kobani, a massive explosion tore through the stillness. The ground heaved violently, jolting Arjan awake with a gasp. Shockwaves pummeled his flimsy tent, nearly ripping it from its moorings and threatening to hurl him from his cot. Heart pounding, he staggered out of his tent into the chaos. His ears rang and his mind reeled, struggling to process the unfolding terror. Around him, Kurdish fighters scrambled in a frenzied panic, narrowly escaping the voracious flames that engulfed several tents. Thick plumes of smoke billowed into the air, smothering the first rays of sunlight. Moments later, another explosion rocked the camp's entrance, followed by the staccato bursts of enemy gunfire that whipped up a blinding dust storm across the base.

Arjan darted between collapsing debris and disoriented fighters, his breath ragged with fear.

"Sahin! Sahin!" he screamed, his voice cracking as he pushed forward. His gaze swept over the carnage, searching desperately for any sign of her. Each step carried him further into the blaze, driven by a primal need to find her.

The dense haze was suffocating, its acrid bite stinging his eyes and searing his throat. Suddenly, a sickening crunch underfoot made him freeze – a comrade, reduced to blackened char. The gruesome sight churned his stomach, and he gagged, clamping a hand over his mouth to hold it back.

Dizziness crashed over him, and just as his knees buckled, a strong, calloused hand gripped his arm. "Arjan!" Sahin's familiar voice pierced the chaos, steadying him.

Relief washed over him as he looked up. "I was looking for you," he gasped. "Are… are you okay?"

"You need to get to safety," Sahin insisted, pulling him upright. Her gaze shifted past him, locking onto Nasrin emerging through the smoke. "Nasrin!" Sahin called decisively. "Take him to the bunker. I need to rally the fighters. *Now!*"

Nasrin nodded, moving swiftly to his side.

"Have you seen Awira?" Sahin asked, her eyes scanning the battlefield.

"She was near the sniper tower last I saw," Nasrin replied.

Sahin nodded sharply. Preparing to dash off, she paused to look back. "Arjan! Stay in the bunker. Do not come out, no matter what," she instructed firmly.

Arjan met her gaze, the severity of the moment rendering him speechless. He nodded silently, his throat tight with emotion, as Nasrin guided him toward the relative safety of the bunker. With a final glance, Sahin sprinted away, disappearing into the swirling smoke.

Inside the shelter, Nasrin turned to him, "Are you okay?"

Arjan nodded numbly, his mind a blur. Nasrin handed him a flask, "Drink. It'll help."

Grateful, Arjan sipped the water and wiped his mouth. His eyes lingered on the young warrior, her calm demeanor defying the bedlam outside.

"I have to go now. Stay here – this bunker is safe. Do not come out under any circumstances." Nasrin said calmly.

As she turned to leave, Arjan felt a flush of embarrassment. Here he was, seeking refuge while she was ready to face the storm. "Good luck, Nasrin! Stay safe," he murmured.

She gave a firm nod before vanishing back into the fray.

Meanwhile, Sahin climbed the sniper tower for a vantage point. Scanning the battlefield, her eyes widened in horror as a main battle tank rumbled toward their base. "Daesh is coming with a tank!" she shouted, her voice resounding across the base.

Dread rippled through the Kurdish ranks. Sahin yanked back the scope, her crosshairs flitting across the parched landscape. Through the lens, she spotted ISIS gunmen holed up in civilian buildings, lying in wait like pit vipers.

"Our light weapons can't take out the tank. I'll get someone on the turret!" Awira yelled.

"Too dangerous! They'll blow it apart!" Sahin countered.

"We have no choice – it's the only anti-tank weapon we've got!" Awira insisted.

"We need to neutralize their shooters first; they're providing cover for the tank," Sahin reasoned.

Kurdish gunners took cover behind sandbag emplacements, locking into a fierce firefight with the enemy shooters. Sahin's marksmanship shone as she took down two combatants. But their counterfire was swiftly snuffed out, like a candle in a gale. The tank rumbled closer, unleashing a devastating barrage of shells that carved through encampments. Six fighters were killed, many more lay wounded, their cries echoing through the haze-choked air.

In a fit of rage, Eylo seized a grenade launcher and scaled the watchtower. Balancing the weapon on his shoulder, he took aim at the tank.

"Eylo, get down! Don't be reckless!" Zoran shouted.

His warning was drowned out by the roar of a shell as it struck the watchtower. The Kurds watched in horror as Eylo disappeared into the inferno. The flaming tower cast an ominous hue over their stricken faces as the tank pressed forward, relentless in its advance.

Sitting the war out in the sterile hush of the bunker, Arjan felt the walls closing in. Isolated from the fray, his ignorance of the battlefield only swelled his anxiety. He didn't want to let Sahin down by disobeying her instructions, but intrusive thoughts gnawed at him. With a resolute breath, Arjan clambered out of the bunker, ready to face whatever lay beyond.

Stepping into the open, the scale of destruction hit him like a blow. Half of their forces lay dead or wounded, and their once-secure positions were now smoldering ruins. Yet, despite the overwhelming odds, the Kurds refused to go down without a fight. Their defiance lit a fire within Arjan, his fear hardening into steely determination.

Zoran and Asos hunkered down in their sandbag nest, launching intermittent sorties at the enemy. Each time the tank paused to reload, Sahin leaned out, methodically picking off enemy snipers. Awira and the other gunners provided cover fire to protect her. Despite their efforts, frustration surged as the enemy snipers seemed endless. They kept popping up non-stop like video game bots, wave after wave.

The tank, a monstrous metal behemoth, rumbled ever closer, its mechanical growl pulsing through the ground. With each advance, it loomed larger, a terrifying spectre of impending doom that threatened to crush them any moment.

"We can't hold out forever. We've got to take out the goddamn tank," Awira roared, her voice taut with desperation. "We're sitting ducks!"

"Comrade Sahin! Let me deploy the turret," Nasrin implored, eager to engage.

Sahin's gaze flickered between Nasrin's fervent plea and the turret's exposed position. "The moment you man it, you'll be a target. The snipers or the tank will take you out."

Awira, her patience frayed, snapped, "Unless we break their coordination, they are invincible!"

Asos growled, throwing up his hands. "Where the hell are the American jets when you need them?"

At the bunker entrance, Arjan overheard their tense exchange. His eyes, drawn to the colourful graffiti on the nearby wall and the spray paint cans strewn beneath it, sparked with an inspiration. "Sahin! I've got an idea," he called out, emboldened by the urgency of the moment.

Sahin whipped around, her stormy gray eyes narrowing. "Arjan! What the hell are you doing out here? Get back inside!"

But Arjan stood his ground. "Remember how we blinded the Armenian squad with those spray bombs? Maybe we can…"

"We don't have time for this, Arjan," Sahin snapped, her voice clipped.

Awira, intrigued, cut in, "Wait! He might be onto something. We can't destroy the tank, but what if we blind it? Throw them into disarray?"

"Exactly!" Arjan exclaimed, his voice gaining conviction.

"But how? We don't have smoke bombs," Nasrin pointed out.

"Doesn't matter. Those tanks have thermal sights," Sahin added, dismissing the idea entirely.

Undeterred, Arjan pressed on, "What if we use Nasrin's spray cans? They're highly combustible. The exploding paint could impair the tank's vision, even if just for a moment. We just need the right aim – or a bit of luck."

"C'mon, Arjan! We can't bank on miracles," Sahin retorted.

"If you think it's a long shot, how about we mix them with grenades?" Nasrin proposed. "At the very least, the explosion will be bigger."

"What's with the sudden obsession with spray cans? That tank will ride them out without a hitch," Sahin countered.

"Either way, it could create the diversion we need to deploy the turret. After all, that's our only real shot," Nasrin said.

"It's worth a shot. Do you have a better plan, Sahin?" Awira pressed.

Sahin hesitated, her eyes on the approaching tank. After a tense silence, she gave a reluctant nod. "If the commander thinks it'll work, who am I to argue?"

"Alright! Here goes nothing. C'mon everyone!" Awira declared, rounding up fighters to assist Arjan with the preparations.

At the frontline, Zoran noticed fighters abandoning their posts, scrambling for paint cans. "What the hell is going on? What are they doing?" he burst out in frustration.

Fighters clustered around Arjan and Ron, hastily binding grenades to aerosol cans. Awira approached with another crate, her voice ragged but resolute. "Mix and match, everyone. Let's cook up a miracle."

Zoran watched in disbelief as seasoned fighters armed themselves with paint cans. "Who put Mr Gamer in charge of this fucking battle?" he sputtered. "Stop indulging his crazy ideas. We are all going to get killed!"

Awira shot him a calm but cutting look. "There's no time for dissent. Please cooperate; the plan might just save us."

Zoran scoffed, incredulous. "I cannot believe it. A veteran like you falling for this farce? Commander, please!"

Inside the tank, the rattle of machinery filled the hull as it trudged forward. Abu, the driver, peered through his viewport, noting the abrupt silence from the Kurds. "Have they run away?" he asked, hope tinged with suspicion.

Hamza, the commander, studied the tactical display with sharp focus. His experience with the Kurds told him they weren't the type to back down. "That's surprising," he responded thoughtfully, his eyes never leaving the screen. "Or maybe they're setting up an ambush."

He grabbed the walkie-talkie, tuning to the frequency of the infantry unit stationed behind them. "Zaka, can you spot the enemies?" he inquired.

After a brief pause, Zaka's voice crackled over the static of the radio. "Negative. No movement."

Meanwhile, the Kurdish fighters had stealthily spread along the trenches, clutching grenades and paint cans. On cue, they hurled the improvised projectiles, bracing for what might be an ingenious ploy or a spectacular failure. The battlefield erupted with bursts of explosions and sizzling paint, swathing the area around the tank in flames. When the pressurized cans met fire, they catapulted into tiny, erratic missiles. Most detonated into raging fireballs, while others zipped around wildly. Despite the visual frenzy, the tank continued its steady advance, barely affected by the fireworks.

From his cover, Zoran peeked at the unfolding spectacle. "Did you really think paintballing a tank would stop it?" he scoffed bitterly.

Encased within the tank's soundproof, armored shell, the impact of the paint cans and grenades felt as inconsequential as pebbles against a fortress. Inside, the enemy crew smirked. The Kurds' desperation appeared trivial, almost comical to them.

"Looks like someone's brought pebbles to a tank fight," Hamza remarked dryly, shaking his head at what he assumed was either desperation or depleted ammunition. "Surge ahead. Let's finish them off," he ordered, his confidence unshaken.

The Kurds looked on in growing despair as their last-ditch effort crumbled before their eyes. But just as hope dwindled, the tank lurched to a halt. Confusion swept through the ranks, quickly giving way to tentative joy.

Miraculously, a few spray cans had hit their mark. Thick, vibrant splashes of primer now smeared the tank's viewports and optical periscope, blinding its electronic eyes.

"Woah! I can't believe it actually worked… look!" Ron exclaimed, his voice filled with astonishment and relief.

The breakthrough was a shot in the arm for the deflated troops, spurring them to reclaim their positions. As his plan worked flawlessly, Arjan felt a surge of redemption. In the shadow of death, instinct led him to the only resource he knew – what once seemed like fiction had, in that moment, become a blueprint for survival.

"Nasrin, take the turret. Hurry, hurry! Everyone else, focus on the shooters!" Awira commanded.

"Move fast! We don't have much time before they recover," Sahin urged.

As the Kurdish gunners laid down suppressive fire, Nasrin scrambled into the anti-tank turret and unleashed its firepower, jolting the sleeping beast of a weapon to life. For the first time, the tank faced a genuine threat, its impenetrable façade rattled by the rapid-fire onslaught.

Inside the tank, agitation swirled, "What the fuck is happening? Why are we blinded?" Hamza shouted at Abu.

In a frantic bid to regain operational visibility, Abu toggled the display to thermal sights. The screen only showed distorted, garbled heat signatures. "We've got a complete vision failure," he reported, panic edging his voice as he slammed the accelerator.

Hamza, gone berserk, retaliated with blind-fire shelling. The tank jerked forward, firing wildly. Most shells crashed into the open ground, but one narrowly missed Sahin's tower.

Unflinching, Sahin kept her focus on the enemy snipers, picking them off one by one as their numbers dwindled.

Nasrin capitalized on the critical window of opportunity, directing a concentrated stream of fire at the disoriented tank. Amid the barrage, a loud crack rang out as the tank's caterpillar tracks snapped. The colossal vehicle halted to a dead stop – a mobility kill.

Inside, Hamza's desperation reached a fever pitch. "Get out there and report the enemy turret's coordinates!" he barked at Abu.

Abu froze, his face drained of colour.

"Don't be a coward! Move it. We're dead meat if we stay blind," Hamza snarled.

Abu's body trembled as he reluctantly stood up. He opened the commander's hatch and stuck his neck out. Bullets zipped past as he quickly scanned the battlefield, relaying the turret's position back to his commander.

As Abu tried to slide back into the tank, Hamza blocked him. "You want to deny your passage to Jannah? Stay up and man the machine gun. Don't be a coward! Fight till your last breath!" he ordered coldly, nearly shoving him back into position.

Resigned to his fate, Abu obeyed, firing indiscriminately. The Kurds, caught off-guard, scrambled for cover. Asos, unable to retreat in time, was riddled with bullets. Zoran screamed in anguish, dragging his comrade's bloodied body to cover. Arjan watched in stunned silence, pride collapsing into crushing regret.

Before Abu could inflict further damage, Nasrin took precise aim and fired. The gunner crumpled forward, motionless. Inside the tank, Hamza spat a curse. With a swift, almost callous shove, he pushed Abu's corpse out of the hatch and slammed it shut.

Nasrin resumed her relentless assault on the crippled tank. Inside, Hamza desperately tried to align the main gun toward her position.

"Nasrin! Get down and take cover," Sahin yelled from her post.

"I can't back down now, sister!" Nasrin shouted; her voice tight. "I almost have him. It's now or never!"

"The barrel is aimed right at you. Can't you see it?" Sahin urged, her voice thick with panic.

"I know! But if I stop now, we'll have nothing left to destroy it," Nasrin shot back, her war cry fierce as she pressed on, eyes burning with resolve, finger steady on the trigger.

Under Nasrin's barrage, the tank finally succumbed – flames burst from its interior, and critical-damage alarms blared. Inside, Hamza was gripped by the cold claws of panic as he confronted his impending fate.

The sight of the burning tank sparked a moment of triumph among the Kurds. But it was short-lived. A final shell from the tank struck the turret, unleashing a wave of terror through the ranks. The explosion sent Nasrin's charred body crashing to the ground.

Hamza, seizing the chaos, abandoned the burning tank and fled for his life, while the remaining enemy forces retreated in disarray.

Spotting Hamza's escape, Awira called to Sahin, "You've got a clear shot at their ringleader. Don't let him get away!"

Sahin, reeling from the shock, took a moment to process Awira's warning. She gathered herself and scoped the battlefield, but her tears clouded her precision. Her first shot missed, whizzing past Hamza as he sprinted. Her hands trembled, and she quickly adjusted her aim, but the weight of the tragedy had completely thrown her off. The second shot also went wide, allowing Hamza to dive into an open drain and disappear.

Frustrated, Sahin flung her rifle aside and climbed down. She rushed to Nasrin, who lay mutilated on the ground, surrounded by Arjan, Ron, and Awira, their faces wet with tears. Sahin knelt, cradling Nasrin's head in her lap. "Nasrin, my sister… no… nooo…" she sobbed, her grief pouring out.

Nasrin's eyes flickered weakly, a faint glimmer of recognition passing between them before her breathing stilled, and her eyes glazed over. Sahin's cries deepened as she pressed Nasrin tightly to her chest.

As the smoke cleared, the Kurds were left to confront a hollow and a pyrrhic victory. Heartbroken, they moved slowly through the rubble, searching for their fallen comrades. The bitter cost of their hard-fought battle lingered heavily in the air, reminding them of the sacrifices made and the lives altered forever.

* * *

Following the attack, there was no time for grief or healing. The surviving fighters, acutely aware of their marked fate and the threat of another assault, dedicated themselves to preparing funerals for their fallen comrades. The grim task of recovering the dead fell upon them, made all the more harrowing by the condition of the bodies. Many were disfigured and scattered across the battlefield, requiring a painstaking effort to gather the remnants. Each search and retrieval of those who had once stood bravely beside them struck deep into their hearts. Hands trembled and breaths faltered as they shouldered the heavy burden of this sombre duty. Amid the endless gloom, a haunting thought secretly lingered among the survivors: perhaps those who had perished were the fortunate ones. They, at least, would receive the dignity of a proper farewell. A sacred closure that seemed increasingly unlikely for those who remained.

As the sun dipped below the horizon, bathing the ravaged base in a melancholic light, the fighters assembled beneath the singed branches of an ancient olive tree. Scarred from countless battles, the tree stood as a voiceless sentinel over a series of freshly dug graves. With reverence, the fighters lowered the shrouded remains into their final resting places. Hands lifted toward the fading light, they chanted a funeral prayer, their voices rising in a haunting melody that echoed across the quiet field. One by one, the fighters stepped forward to pay their respects. They placed small tokens on the earthen mounds – stones, flowers, and scraps of fabric from their battle fatigues, each a personal tribute to a lost companion. Mutual condolences were exchanged in hushed tones, marking a tearful farewell yet a bittersweet privilege, as it ensured that their brothers and sisters in arms were honoured before the storm resumed.

The ISIS onslaught had devastated their ranks and reduced the base to rubble. Collapsed buildings, razed sleeping tents, and an empty armory painted a grim picture. The lone turret lay beyond repair, a silent relic of their battered defences. Yet, the Kurds pressed on, salvaging what little they could. Zoran, Awira, and Sahin worked tirelessly to rebuild defensive positions, hauling and stacking sandbags, while others mended the shattered boundary walls.

That night, the fighters huddled around an old CRT TV and watched the news. The world had already written Kobani's obituary. Experts spoke of the resistance as a lost cause, their hope extinguished long before the final battle.

On FNBC News, the Pentagon delivered a grim prognosis. "Kobani will likely fall to the terrorists," the press secretary stated, his tone resigned. "Airstrikes alone are insufficient. We are looking beyond Kobani until a viable ground strategy develops in Syria."

The room fell silent, the weight of their predicament palpable.

Awira entered, sensing the despair. Without a word, she turned off the TV. "Let's eat," she said, her tone resolute.

In the dining area, the fighters sat on the floor and quietly nibbled on meagre portions. No one spoke of wargaming strategies or future as an eerie silence hung over the base, reflective of their weary spirits.

As night deepened, the fighters sought rest under a makeshift tarpaulin roof. While many tried to sleep, the quiet was filled with the sound of restless shifting. Others lay awake, staring at the stars or lost in the faces of loved ones in cherished photographs, clutching them close against the chill of the night air.

In the nearly bombed-out command room, Arjan sat before a battered computer. The screen, though cracked, flickered to life. He wiped the webcam's lens with a careful swipe, his fingers tentative on the fragile machine. As he adjusted the microphone, its stand scraped against the rubble-strewn desk. Despite the soot and scars etched into his face, he couldn't muster the care to tidy his dishevelled appearance. As the livestream began, he forced a semblance of composure. "It was my dream to become a popular streamer," he began, his voice steady despite the emotion in his eyes. "A million subscribers. I still can't believe it. Thank you for making it come true."

Arjan paused to take a deep breath. After a moment of silence, he continued, "But none of it matters anymore. All my dreams and aspirations, once so vivid, now feel hollow. I've started valuing the little things – the ease of a deep breath, the serene beauty of a sunset, the chirping of birds. Simple joys we take for granted until they're at risk of being stolen away. Sadly, I've realized their worth far too late." He clenched his jaw, biting his lip to steady the quiver of tears threatening to fall.

"We're surrounded by ISIS. Every escape route has been cut off. They've sworn to hold their afternoon prayer tomorrow in Kobani's grand mosque, right next to our base. They plan to capture us within the next fifteen hours, and sadly, there's not much we can do to stop it."

The video had been live for barely two minutes, yet its impact spread across the globe.

Arjan's voice, urgent and raw, resonated far and wide. In Germany, Eitan clenched his phone, knuckles white with tension. In Saudi Arabia, Faiz sat motionless at his desk, tears blurring his vision.

Arjan's words rippled like a shockwave, cutting across borders and screens. "US-led airstrikes have helped but haven't stopped ISIS's advance. What we really needed were boots on the ground."

Farther away in Pakistan, his message struck a chord even with the youngest viewers. Zafar watched the live feed with his family, tears brimming in his eyes. His elder daughter, sensing his sorrow, wrapped her arms around him in a comforting embrace.

"Turkey could have helped us, but they've kept their borders closed despite countless global appeals. Today's attack has left us more vulnerable than ever – we've run out of soldiers, guns, ammunition, and supplies to hold ISIS off any longer," Arjan explained.

In a sparse New Delhi office, Officer Khan and Joginder watched the stream on a small TV. The fan hummed softly as Khan leaned forward, brow furrowed, his sharp gaze tempered by reflection. Silence filled the room.

"Though food and water are scarce, our resolve is stronger than ever," Arjan said firmly. "We won't go down without a fight. As they say, it's better to burn out in battle than fade away in surrender."

Public opinion erupted, hailing Arjan as an unlikely hero – an outsider caught in a foreign war, now a reluctant symbol of defiance. His video transcended digital platforms, airing across global media as if it were a plea from a head of state. Around the world, people gathered in streets, offices, cafes, and homes, riveted by the story of a man standing firm with his comrades and the love of his life against impossible odds.

As Arjan neared the video's end, his shoulders slumped slightly, a tremor in his voice betraying the composure he fought to maintain. "This could be my last video," he rasped, a choked sob escaping his lips.

"This is my final goodbye to my viewers, my family, and my friends. The time has come to drop the camera and pick up the gun."

Arjan's words washed over his family in a quiet living room. Anita sat frozen, her hands clasped over her mouth as tears streamed down her cheeks. Beside her, Rajesh remained stoic, a pillar of restrained emotion, silently lending his wife strength to endure the unbearable. At their feet, Mario lay listlessly, sensing the sorrow engulfing their home.

On the television, a news channel relayed Arjan's live video, the ticker scrolling beneath his image: *Indian Braveheart's Emotional Last Video.*

Arjan took a moment, his eyes closing briefly as if gathering the courage to voice his next words. "To my parents," he began, his voice cracking under the weight of guilt, "I'm so sorry. I wish I had been a better son. I wish I hadn't been so selfish." He took a shaky breath, the longing palpable in his tone. "I still hope to make you proud in some small way. Please forgive me, Mummy, Papa. I love you…. And I know you'll take good care of Mario."

17
Battle Royale

D-Day, 1st November, 2014

The morning hung heavy with an overcast sky, casting a dim light over the Kurdish fighters who had been on high alert since dawn. After a sleepless night, their vigilance was beginning to fray under the crushing weight of an inevitable attack. Subtle yet unmistakable movements at the outskirts confirmed their fears – the oppressor was returning to settle unfinished business, steadfast in its menacing promise. Behind their fortifications, the fighters watched with mounting dread as ISIS shooters emerged from the haze. As Awira marshaled her troops to brace for what appeared to be a highly coordinated attack, ISIS abruptly unleashed its secret weapon. From the heights of Mistanour Hill, two up-armored SUVs roared into view, barreling toward the base.

"They are Daesh's suicide-battalion. They're sending SVBIEDs to clear the way before the final push," Sahin explained urgently.

"What? SVBIEDs? What are those?" Arjan asked, apprehension creeping into his voice.

"Car bombs designed to explode among us," Sahin clarified.

"Suicide bombers on wheels? How twisted is that?" Ron interjected, his tone taut with disbelief.

Arjan stared in horror at the oncoming vehicles, struggling to hold back a sob.

Lacking an air force, ISIS had turned to the next most lethal alternative – SVBIEDs, or suicide vehicle-borne improvised explosive devices, often called 'poor man's cruise missiles.' These crude yet devastating weapons allowed ISIS to deliver catastrophic payloads with human drivers on one-way missions. These SUVs, which looked as if they'd rolled straight out of *Mad Max*, were originally civilian cars, now retrofitted into war machines. They were overhauled with welded metal plates, and packed with tons of explosives, capable of swallowing everything within hundreds of metres.

Noticing the fear in her troops' eyes at the approaching ironclad coffins, Awira grabbed the megaphone and drew a deep breath.

"Shervanên Kurdistan!" she called out, her voice booming powerfully across the battlefield. "It doesn't matter how many they are or what weapons they bring. They may have deadlier machines, but these are our streets – our home. We know every corner, every alley, better than they ever will, because we played here as children, and now we defend them as warriors."

Her voice grew stronger, feeding on the determination around her. "They may have firepower, but our vengeance burns brighter. As long as that fire rages in our hearts, we will not falter. We fight for our families, our fallen, and the land that raised us. Let our bullets rain down on them and show them – *this is Kurdish soil. It will never be theirs!*" she ended with a cry of defiance.

Awira's stirring words swept through the ranks like wildfire. The fighters stood taller, their fear melting into resolve. As one, they roared, "*Bijî Kurdistan*!"

The thunderous battle cry echoed across the base, galvanizing them as they gripped their weapons tightly and fixed their gazes on the enemy. Energized and determined, they quickly dispersed to their battle stations, ready to defend their homeland.

"Awira! Engage the SUVs. I'll handle the shooters!" Sahin shouted over the din.

Her Zagros rifle cracked crisply as she picked off enemy snipers, creating a crucial opening for the Kurdish gunners. Meanwhile, Arjan and Ron, driven by desperation, emptied their magazines at the SUVs thundering down the dirt road. Yet, their bullets met only the harsh clang of metal, deflected by the slat-armour bolted onto the windshields and engines. The absence of anti-tank weaponry was glaring, as the armored vehicles, nearly impervious to small arms fire, bore down on them. Their courage, though fierce, seemed woefully inadequate against the onslaught. The determination sparked by Awira's speech began to flicker, and the battle teetered on the edge of a swift and bloody rout at the hands of ISIS.

A sonic boom split the sky, pulling every gaze upward in a rush of hope. Slicing through the clouds, F-16 fighter jets descended like a deus ex machina.

"Oh my God! The Americans are finally here!" Zoran exclaimed, his voice brimming with relief.

"God bless America," Awira declared, her voice imbued with a hope reborn. "They didn't abandon us after all."

The roaring jets brought the kamikaze SUVs to an abrupt halt, while ISIS snipers scattered into the shadows. A wave of exhilaration swept through the Kurdish ranks as the jets, etching brilliant white contrails across the dreary skies, pierced the oppressive gloom.

"Thank god… they truly are a godsend," Arjan whispered to Sahin, their eyes glistening with tears of gratitude.

The jets swooped in a majestic low pass over the ISIS positions, the glow of their white-hot afterburners illuminating the awestruck faces of the Kurds.

Startled by the sudden aerial threat, ISIS fighters froze, like rabbits caught in headlights. Their advance came to a complete halt as though the hand of God had pressed the pause button on an unforgiving showdown, affording the Kurds a precious moment of reprieve.

Hovering directly over ISIS positions, the F-16s cast dark shadows below. Paralyzed by fear, the terrorists cowered, hoping to evade the predatory gaze of the circling jets. The Kurds watched with bated breath, each heart pounding in unison, desperate for the jets to unleash their fury.

On cue, the air thrummed with the sound of missile locks, signaling imminent fireworks. But just as the tension climaxed, it abruptly dissolved. The jets broke formation, rolling sharply before soaring back into the sky without firing a single shot. The anticlimactic departure left the Kurdish faction in stunned silence.

Awira, swept up in despair, flailed her arms and ran after the retreating jets. "Where are you going? Come back. Don't leave us!" she cried, her voice breaking as she collapsed to her knees. It stung like a cruel joke – salvation dangled before them only to be snatched away.

Sahin picked up her sniper scope, scanning the enemy lines with urgency. Her heart sank as she spotted Kurdish flags waving atop enemy buildings. "They've tricked the Americans," she groaned. "They're using our flags to fool the pilots into thinking those are our positions. Unbelievable!"

"They've even camouflaged their SUVs to look like ours… look," Zoran said, shaking his head as he studied the enemy lines.

Sahin nodded grimly.

Arjan tried to inject hope. "I'm sure they'll come around. The Americans will see through this trickery."

"They might," Sahin replied, her tone heavy, "but by then, it'll be too late. We're on our own. Let's not cling to false hope."

As the jet engines faded into the distance, ISIS shooters emerged from hiding and retook their positions. The engines of the kamikaze SUVs roared back to life, each rev brimming with violent intent. ISIS gunners unleashed a barrage of suppressive fire onto the base. Unchallenged, the first bomb-laden Chevrolet Equinox rammed into the fortified boundary wall like a battering ram. Kurdish fighters dove to the ground, bracing for impact as the car detonated, obliterating part of the wall. In deadly synchrony, another SUV followed, its explosion demolishing the weakened boundary. The adjacent bunker crumbled under the shockwave, claiming the lives of seven Kurdish fighters.

Before the dust could settle, the ground shuddered once more as three main battle tanks rolled onto the cratered battlefield. It was an overkill, a grotesque flexing of might against an already broken enemy. ISIS sought to snuff out any remaining embers of Kurdish courage before crushing their corporeal forms.

"It's time to meet our maker!" Sahin declared. "We fight to our last breath and our last bullet. We will not be taken alive. Let's go."

Barely twenty fighters remained, yet their spirits refused to break. The women assisted each other in strapping on suicide vests for one last hurrah – a grim pact sealed with silent nods.

Arjan approached Sahin, his eyes welling with tears as she prepared her own vest. "Sahin, this isn't right. We can't just throw our lives away. There surely has to be another way. We can't just give up."

"Any Yazidi girl would choose death over capture by Daesh," Sahin replied, her voice firm.

"But it doesn't have to end like this!" Arjan pleaded, his voice breaking.

"We've always known this day might come and we have always been prepared. You will not understand, Arjan," Sahin said, her tone laced with bittersweet determination. "But we will make them pay dearly before we fall."

Just then, an enemy tank shell screamed overhead, striking the last standing sniper tower. The structure erupted in a fiery blast, raining debris across the base. A jagged shard of shrapnel tore through the chaos, slicing into Sahin's shoulder and sending her crumpling to the ground.

"Sahin!" Arjan shouted, anguish twisting his voice. He rushed to her side, lifting her into his arms. "Are you okay?" he asked, his words trembling as he scanned her injury.

Sahin, dazed and in shock, barely responded as Arjan carried her to the shelter of a large concrete block amid the rubble. She winced, blood seeping from her shoulder. Arjan gently laid her down, cushioning her head in his lap. He tore a strip of cloth from his shirt and tightly bandaged her wound, desperate to staunch the bleeding. "Stay with me, Sahin!" he pleaded, his hands trembling as he pressed down, fighting to suppress the terror rising within him.

Sahin's eyes fluttered open, her expression hardening with resilience despite the pain. "We fight to the end, Arjan," she rasped.

In the distance, engines roared louder as more fighters in armored trucks surged toward them from the west, near the Yumurtalık border crossing. Some of these camouflaged vehicles bore Kurdish flags.

"They're surrounding us!" Zoran shouted, his voice sharp and urgent.

The grim news spread among the surviving fighters, leaving them resigned to the tightening noose of their fates. Arjan's eyes filled with tears as he looked down at Sahin, her calm gaze meeting his.

"Help me up, Arjan," Sahin said, attempting to sit. The agony, however, was too great.

"No," Arjan said firmly, his voice breaking. "We'll stay together. If this is the end, we'll face it in each other's arms."

Sahin remained silent, her face serene. Slowly, she raised a trembling hand and wiped away Arjan's tears, her touch soothing even in the midst of their suffering. "I told you to leave, Arjan. This… this was never your fight…" she murmured between laboured breaths.

Arjan reached into his pocket and pulled out a diamond ring. Taking her calloused hand in his, he slipped it onto her finger. Sahin's eyes brimmed with tears.

"I'm not waiting for the next life," Arjan said, his voice faltering. "I love you, Sahin." His whisper broke as tears rolled down his cheeks.

"I love you too," she replied softly.

Arjan wrapped his arms around her, holding on tight as if their warmth could push back the cold despair gripping them. He leaned down, pressing a soft kiss to her forehead – a promise that they would face whatever came next together. They lay in the lap of the devastation, surrounded by the remnants of a world torn apart, yet somehow finding solace in each other's presence. Even as chaos swirled around them, their bond felt unshakeable – a love that could withstand even the darkest of times.

Suddenly, a missile streaked from a pick-up truck on the west side of the base. The Kurds dropped to their knees, but the warhead surged over their heads and tore into an ISIS tank in a fiery explosion. The Kurds watched in disbelief.

Awira sprang to her feet and scoped the firing army, astonished by the revelation. "They're allies!" she exclaimed. "It's the Peshmerga!"

The Peshmerga's artillery thundered again, setting another tank ablaze. ISIS, taken completely by surprise, had not anticipated resistance – let alone a counterattack of this scale.

Awira rushed to Sahin, who was propped up against a concrete block, with Arjan at her side. Crouching next to her, Awira's voice was urgent. "The Peshmerga are here. They've got anti-tank weapons," she said.

Sahin nodded, a faint smile crossing her face despite the pain. "Looks like we've got an extra life," she replied, her voice steady with determination. "Let's make it count."

Bolstered by Sahin's resolve, Awira spurred into action, rallying the fighters back into assault positions. As the Peshmerga delivered precise strikes on the remaining tank, Kurdish forces turned their focus to eliminating ISIS gunners. Under fire from two fronts, ISIS found itself in a chokehold. All three tanks were reduced to smoldering wrecks. The turnaround revived the Kurdish fighters' spirits, their cheers filling the air.

Hamza, the ISIS commander, seethed at his routing troops. "Bloody cowards!" he roared, his bloodshot eyes burning with fury. He quickly rounded up his most trusted men. Pointing toward a group of armored SUVs, he barked, "Load them with explosives – everything we've got. UXOs, oil, shrapnel – pack them all in!"

The fighters scrambled to comply, heaping volatile materials onto the already deadly payloads.

Zaka, the infantry commander, stepped forward, his expression tense. "Hamza, this is madness. They've got reinforcements. We need to regroup and return later."

"No!" Hamza snarled, dismissing him with a sharp wave. "This is our chance to finish off that hellcat and her imbecile unit. They die today. We will get our revenge!"

"They've bolstered their forces, we must reconsider," Zaka pressed.

"Not yet. The base is exposed, and the enemy hasn't consolidated. This is our window," Hamza retorted, his gaze fixed on the Peshmerga positions still separated from the Kurdish base.

Overriding caution, Hamza rallied the *fedayeen* for their mission. "Prove your worth to Allah! Drive fast, overrun the infidels before they regroup… go go!" he commanded in Arabic, his voice sharp with chilling intensity.

The fedayeen, four fighters in all, chanted in unison as they took the wheels of four explosive-laden SUVs. "*Allahu Akbar wal izzatu lillah!* We won't let our brothers' martyrdom go to waste!" they proclaimed, their voices resonating with zeal.

Zaka, angered by Hamza's defiance, warned, "Hamza! This is suicidal."

"Really? What else did you think I built a suicide-battalion for?" Hamza shot back.

As the SUVs revved up, Hamza headed straight for the weapons cache, retrieving a sealed plastic bag from the vault.

Zaka's apprehension spiked. "Have you lost your mind? The command has not sanctioned its use. You cannot deploy that," he exclaimed.

"Go ahead. Report me," Hamza taunted. "And while you're at it, don't forget to regale them with the legends of your unit's cowardly retreat," he added, his provocations biting as he hefted the ominous bag into the boot of an armored Toyota Land Cruiser. Muttering under his breath, he sneered, "This will take care of all of them – even the survivors."

Zaka's voice trembled with dread, "This will have serious repercussions."

"If we don't crush them today, they will only grow stronger," Hamza countered.

"You've lost your mind," Zaka muttered, his hands balling into fists of frustration.

Hamza gave a final, mocking salute, "See you on the other side." Sliding into the driver's seat, he declared fervently, "Inshallah! My explosion will have the greatest impact on the apostates." Leaning out of the window, he shouted, "May Allah accept us in Jannah!"

On his cue, the fedayeen slammed their pedals to the floor, their SUVs hurtling toward the Kurdish base. All at once.

The Peshmerga hastily loaded and fired their anti-tank munitions, but to little avail. The missiles plunged into dirt, failing to lock onto the rapidly moving targets. Panic rippled through the Peshmerga forces, unprepared for such high-speed threats.

"These cars are moving too fast for anti-tank weaponry to hit with precision," Awira lamented.

With no other option, the Kurdish infantry directed a barrage of gunfire at the oncoming SUVs. Like before, the armored SUVs pushed forward with impunity, undeterred by the light arms onslaught.

Closing in at 800 metres, the suicide bombers tightened into a militaristic diamond formation. Hamza nestled his Land Cruiser at the core, shielded on all sides by the armored vehicles. Like a kamikaze motorcade of sorts.

"They're protecting the middle car. It must have the heaviest payload," Zoran analyzed, his breath catching.

Fate intervened. A stray rifle round pierced the metal plate covering the rear tire of the left-flanked SUV. What had once been its protection was now peeled away, exposing its Achilles' heel.

Awira, ever vigilant, spotted the critical vulnerability. "The left car's rear tire is bare open," she called out.

Seizing the chance, the infantry targeted the exposed tire. Bullets shredded through it, sparking violently. The SUV lurched, veering off course and careening into a shell crater. The ramped rim of the abyss catapulted it skyward, flipping end over end like a possessed rag doll. Within seconds, its payload detonated in a monstrous fireball, erupting mid-air and illuminating the battlefield in a blaze of fiery destruction.

"What the hell was that?" one Peshmerga fighter whispered, his voice laced with shock, eyes wide at the spectacle above.

Another fighter, using dark humour to cope with the absurdity of the crash, muttered, "Guess that was ISIS's attempt at a space mission." The offhand remark hung awkwardly, barely masking the brutal reality.

Their survival was anything but certain. Yet, this dramatic takedown felt like a foot in the door, lifting morale and instilling a crucial belief: the armored car bombs could be neutralized.

Taking inspiration from this small victory, the Peshmerga renewed their efforts. They stuck to their anti-tank guns, undaunted by the blistering speed of the enemy vehicles, which made precision targeting all the more difficult.

Missiles streaked across the battlefield; most whistling perilously close but missing their fast-moving targets. Then, with a resounding roar, one missile found its mark, striking an SUV at the convoy's rear. The impact ignited the vehicle, and moments later, a massive secondary explosion erupted from its payload. As smoke billowed, a wave of cheers broke out among the Peshmerga fighters. Their missiles were finally hitting home. With two car bombs destroyed and three still charging, the Peshmerga's grit hardened into steel. They realigned their sights, ready to go for the kill.

Belief, a beautiful and potent weapon, had taken root. The moment they began to trust in their ability to dismantle those car bombs, what once seemed impossible started to unravel before their eyes.

After several misfires, the persistence bore fruit once again. Another warhead screamed across the field, slamming into an SUV on the enemy's right flank. The explosion was fierce, engulfing not just the targeted vehicle but also catching the lead vehicle in its destructive embrace. As a colossal plume of fire and smoke flared, the Land Cruiser burst forth from the flames, unscathed – like a spectre emerging from the ashes. It tore forward in its relentless advance, now a mere 500 metres from the Kurdish base.

The Peshmerga fighters grew frantic as the gap closed. They fired missile after missile, their shots increasingly desperate. One missile nearly struck the Kurdish base itself. Alarmed, the Peshmerga commander raised his hand sharply.

"Hold your fire!" he ordered.

The fighters froze, stunned by the abrupt command.

"That car is too close," the commander warned. "If we keep firing blindly, we risk blowing up our ally's base."

"But that car bomb will kill them!" one fighter protested.

"It's too late," the commander said with chilling finality. "They're already within the blast radius. Even if we were to hit it, it would only make the explosion worse… there's nothing we can do!" he bemoaned.

With heavy hearts, the Peshmerga fighters ceased their assault, watching helplessly from the sidelines as the Land Cruiser closed in.

Awira watched the unfolding horror. Her spirits were crushed; witnessing the Peshmerga, their last hope, forced to stand down and spectate their impending doom. It was a grim signal: this was the end. Glancing at her weary infantry, she saw the same realization mirrored in their faces – ammunition depleted, options exhausted. "This is it. Prepare for the worst," she said.

As Arjan absorbed her ominous words, a sense of déjà vu struck him. Visions of the kamikaze match flashed in his head. He remembered how Zafar had made a similar doomsday call when Sahin faced Vlad charging toward her. Survival had seemed impossible then, too. Yet Sahin had stood her ground, training her sniper on Vlad's helmet. The bullet had sliced through the helmet's eye-slits, killing him instantly. These memories ignited a fire within Arjan, propelling him into action.

On the battlefield, the final kamikaze SUV – the modded Land Cruiser, carrying the deadliest explosives – remained at large, now just 300 metres away. Arjan sprinted to the front line, his heart pounding in his ears, while the Peshmerga observed from a safer distance. Some couldn't bear to look, turning their heads away, their bodies tensing in dread. The Kurds, directly in harm's way, pressed themselves against the dusty earth, murmurs of final prayers threading through their strained breaths.

Arjan snatched up a sniper rifle and planted himself squarely in the SUV's path. He peered through the scope at the tiny glass port – a mere pinhole in the otherwise cage-armored windshield – the fedayeen's lone visual aid. It was a one-in-a-million shot, but what more could he lose? Arjan led the target, swinging the rifle to align with the SUV's trajectory.

"Hope always," he whispered, grasping for a measure of calm, enough to completely still his breath and squeeze the trigger. The weapon's recoil sent a jarring jolt through his arms as the bullet sped away, only to miss its mark.

"Arjan, get down! That's impossible!" Ron yelled, witnessing his friend's audacious attempt. But Arjan was undeterred. Fueled by adrenaline, he hastily reloaded, his hands trembling.

As the SUV closed in, now a mere 150 metres away, Hamza reached for the detonation switch. Just as his finger grazed the trigger, another bullet shattered the tiny glass port and burrowed into his skull. His body jerked backward, slumping lifelessly, his hand drifting away from the fatal switch.

Breathing heavily, Arjan's eyes widened in shock and relief. "The driver is dead," he gasped, the words cutting through the tense air.

Zoran, lying prone, lifted his head in disbelief. "How is that possible?"

But the SUV, unmanned and unstoppable, continued its deadly charge, rapidly closing the remaining distance.

Arjan dropped his rifle and rushed forward, "For God's sake, Commander, trust me this time. We must stop it somehow."

Though still in denial, something in Arjan's impassioned plea snapped Zoran out of his distrust. Instincts kicked in; he stood abruptly and rallied nearby fighters. "Move, build a barricade!" he shouted.

Together, they scrambled, grabbing sandbags from defensive positions and throwing them into the SUV's path. The bags hit the ground with heavy thuds, forming an improvised blockade. The vehicle bucked and swayed against the hastily assembled barriers, the sandbags acting as a flurry of speed breakers, disrupting its momentum. Buoyed by the small victory, the fighters redoubled their resolve, piling on more sandbags and shoring up the barriers feverishly. At last, the Land Cruiser lost all inertia, grinding to a halt just metres from the base.

A heavy silence descended, and the Kurds tentatively raised their heads to witness a twist of fate. The sudden stillness allowed them a moment to absorb the scale of the catastrophe they had just averted. They stared in disbelief at the immobilized car bomb at their gate, which stood like a shackled killer in the courtroom, its sinister plot thwarted, now subdued and awaiting judgment. Without hesitation, Awira and Zoran rushed to disarm the vehicle. As the fighters slowly rose, the weight of their near escape melted into euphoria. Tears of relief and joy streamed down faces as they embraced, celebrating their improbable triumph. From afar, jubilant cheers from the Peshmerga echoed across the battlefield.

Amid the burgeoning celebration, Arjan's eyes sought Sahin. He found her slumped against the charred remains of a tower pole, struggling to stay upright. Her battered sniper rifle, secured with tape, hung limply at her side. Seeing her falter, Arjan's heart clenched. He rushed over, steadying her just as she began to sway.

"Sahin!" he exclaimed softly, his voice laden with deep affection and concern as he gently drew her into a hug. "We survived!"

Together, they stood beside the ruins, their tears mingling as they wept for joy, overwhelmed by gratitude for the reprieve they had been granted.

* * *

The next day, Arjan sat in a bombed-out, roofless room, his heart full as he went live. "To be honest, I thought I'd never see you all again. We had lost all hope. I truly believe my parents' and your prayers played a big role in keeping us alive. We are truly grateful for your support."

Across the globe, people in cafes, homes, salons and workplaces – were riveted, their eyes locked on their phones and TVs, hanging on every word of the vlog.

"I came to Syria on a self-serving pursuit, blind to the true scale of devastation. I was flung into a real war… nothing like the virtual battles I once fought. Seeing it firsthand changed everything. I never expected to witness such resilience – young men and women, guilty of nothing yet fighting for survival. So many lives lost, so much blood spilled – all for a war that should never have been."

In New Delhi, Rajesh and Anita sat glued to their TV, tears brimming as they watched their son with immense pride. Mario rested by their feet, his head tilted in quiet companionship.

Arjan's voice wavered slightly as he continued, "How I wish war were confined to just the fictional realms of video games. There should be no place for such gore in the real world. It's hard to process everything we've seen and experienced, and I wish it didn't have to be this way. Your support has meant everything during this time." With that, he paused, the gravity of his words still echoing, before ending the broadcast.

In the days that followed, the reinforced Kurdish forces unleashed relentless artillery, dismantling ISIS positions and forcing their retreat. The arrival of Peshmerga and intensified coalition airstrikes crippled the enemy's momentum and set the stage for a decisive counterattack. Historically divided by internal strife, the Kurds, many observed, had broken an age-old jinx by uniting against a common threat.

At the heart of this struggle stood Sahin, the revered Kurdish sniper, and Arjan, the Indian vlogger whose gripping footage captivated the world. Their hardscrabble love story went viral, symbolizing the fierce spirit of the resistance and the extraordinary exploits of those fighting for survival.

Epilogue
Hope Always

Three weeks on, Kobani stirred with new life. The battered base had become a budding settlement – fresh tents, new encampments, and half-built mudbrick homes offering shelter to Peshmerga fighters, returning families, and refugees who dared to hope again. Trucks rolled in, laden with food and supplies, their engines mingling with the laughter of barefoot children. Some chased a patched-up soccer ball down dusty alleys, while others, imitating soldiers they'd seen, crouched behind sandbags with toy guns, giggling at their own pretend ambushes. Their joy, fragile yet defiant, felt surreal in a place still bearing deep scars.

Sahin walked beside Arjan, her arm cradled in a sling. At a bend in the gravel path, she paused at the sight of volunteers planting saplings in the cracked soil. Dirt caked their hands as they worked carefully, determined to green the rubble.

"They'll grow," Sahin murmured, almost to herself, a flicker of a smile easing her features with cautious optimism.

Their steps led them to a quiet clearing, where the air grew heavier. A row of graves stretched before them, each marked by a slender olive sapling that swayed in the breeze. Wooden tags bore the names of the fallen – Nasrin, Asos, Eylo, and many others who had paid the ultimate price to give Kobani this moment. Sahin halted at Nasrin's marker, her fingers tracing the carved letters as though reaching for a heartbeat. Her eyes shone, and Arjan stood just behind her, head bowed in silent respect.

The next morning dawned warm and bright. Sahin stepped out in a floral *faqiana*, her sling tucked beneath its folds. Arjan, neatly dressed, joined her as they headed for the makeshift checkpoint. Awira and Zoran stood among half-packed crates of ammunition. Zoran shifted his stance, shooting Arjan a measured look, while Awira folded her arms, her expression unreadable.

"So," Awira said quietly, "you're leaving."

Arjan nodded. "Yes. It's time to go home – my home." He glanced at Sahin, who gave a slow, thoughtful nod.

Awira's gaze flicked back to Sahin. "Everything set? Paperwork, visas…?"

Sahin caught Arjan's eye, and he held up a slim folder in confirmation.

Awira huffed softly, though her expression warmed. "You can't wait to take her away, hmm?" Noticing the flicker of worry in Sahin's face, she softened her tone. "Don't worry about us. We'll be fine. And if we ever need our best shooter, we'll know where to find her."

Sahin's throat tightened. She straightened, giving a crisp salute before Awira pulled her into a hug, lingering a moment longer than usual. Meanwhile, Zoran offered Arjan a slow, stiff handshake – a gesture heavy with reluctant respect.

With farewells said, Arjan and Sahin climbed into a battered jeep. Neighbours and fighters gathered to wave them off. As the engine coughed to life, Sahin turned in her seat one last time, taking in Kobani with a quiet promise in her eyes.

Arjan reached for her hand, giving it a gentle squeeze. "We've got this," he murmured.

She nodded, letting his calm settle over her lingering doubts.

***

Hours later, they settled into their seats on the plane. Through the window, Sahin caught sight of the Erbil International Airport sign, its letters softly aglow in the haze of runway lights.

Next to her, Arjan spoke softly into his phone. "Yes, Mummy, I'll send the flight details, don't worry," he teased. Mid-sentence, he unwrapped a small nasal spray, took a quick spritz, and sighed with relief. "I'll see you in the morning," he finished, glancing at Sahin with a soft, knowing smile.

Ending the call, he noticed his phone buzzing relentlessly – a stream of notifications from the Squad Aces group. With a fond shake of his head at the unending chatter, he switched it to airplane mode and tucked it away.

Turning to Sahin, he held out his hand. She threaded her fingers through his, their touch sure and grounding. Their eyes locked, an intimate silence flowing between them – every scar, every shared memory, every unspoken promise weaving a bond, a silent language only they understood.

The plane's engines roared, and as it lifted into the night, neither let go. In that shared moment, the scars of war seemed distant, and the future glowed with promise. Fingers entwined, hearts set on new beginnings.

◆ ◆ ◆

Three days after D-Day
A news presenter sat poised at the Britain World Media desk, the digital signage behind her illuminating the studio with a muted glow. She faced the camera with a solemn expression.

"A breaking news story is unfolding about a recent cyber shutdown targeting Turkish government websites. The hacktivist group responsible, known as Anonym-Aces, allegedly breached the sites four days ago, holding them for ransom for eighteen hours. Their motive, however, was not financial. An unverified video circulating online features three masked figures delivering demands to Turkish authorities."

The screen cut to the video, where three men in Pinocchio masks stood against a swirling backdrop of binary codes. The footage glitched intermittently, and their voices were distorted to mask their identities as they took turns reading the statement.

The first masked figure began, "We are deeply dissatisfied with Turkey's inaction as the ISIS threat looms over Kobani. While we understand their policy to avoid direct military intervention…"

The second figure continued in a robotic tone, "They cannot block the Peshmerga while their Kurdish brothers and sisters are slaughtered. We demand that Turkey opens its borders immediately – let them defend their own!"

Finally, the third, speaking in a distorted voice, concluded, "In exchange, we pledge not to breach sensitive credentials or data and will restore all hacked websites, ensuring normalcy resumes in Turkey."

The video ended abruptly with a cryptic message flashing across the screen: "No Ace left behind."

Returning to the studio, the presenter resumed, "Anonym-Aces, reportedly based in Saudi Arabia, recently shot to popularity for its cyber-attacks against ISIS, paralyzing their online operations. Turkish government officials, however, dismiss the video as a hoax and insist that these events played no role in their U-turn decision to open borders for Peshmerga forces."

Acknowledgements

Some stories arrive in an instant, others take years to simmer. This one was fuelled by years of gaming and a fascination with the idea that sometimes, life might just imitate play. But no player levels up alone. Every quest, real or virtual, is shaped by those who stand beside us. I am deeply grateful to those who have been part of mine.

To my parents, Dr Shyam Kukreja and Sunita Kukreja – your love, faith, and strength have shaped everything I do. You believed in my dreams even when they seemed unconventional, trusting my journey long before I did. I owe you more than words can ever express.

To my wife, Rishibha – my rock, my partner in everything, and the quiet force behind it all. You've been my fiercest yet most caring critic, always pushing me to never settle for less than my best. This book is as much yours as it is mine.

To my son, Arjan – you are the brightest light in my life. You've filled my world with a love I never knew existed, and being your father is the greatest adventure of all.

To Parina and Rewanth – thank you for always being there, no matter what. And to Ahana and Mivaan, who make up my most lovable little hype team - your excitement and joy remind me why stories matter.

To my family and friends (real and gaming) – your shared experiences, camaraderie, and support have left a lasting mark on this journey, proving that true connection transcends any boundary.

To the team at Srishti Publishers – for believing in this book and bringing it to life with such care and dedication.

And finally, to my readers – thank you for stepping into this world with me. I hope this story stays with you, the way it has lived in me for so long.

With gratitude,
Ritvik Kukreja